Savior

Changing of the Guards

Aquila Thorne

Book 1

Copyright © 2025 Aquila Thorne

All rights reserved

The characters and events portrayed in this book are fictitious. Any similarity to real persons, living or dead, is coincidental and not intended by the author.

No part of this book may be reproduced, or stored in a retrieval system, or transmitted in any form or by any means, electronic, mechanical, photocopying, recording, or otherwise, without express written permission of the publisher.

Savior Changing of the Guards book 1
ISBN-13 : 979-8322153504

Don't read this if the following bothers you
ED
PCOS
Cats
Horses
House fires
Kidnapping
Billionaires
Lots of swearing
Laughing your ass off
Being chained to walls
Alpha protective male
Curvy girls with muffin tops Spicy scenes (not closed door)
Falling in love with a fictional man
Stabby stab (it is after all a Mafia romance)
Old men who wear nothing under their bathrobes
We could go on, but we won't bore you with the details, nor do we want to tell you what the whole book is in a nutshell of trigger warnings!
But you have been warned, so you can't say you haven't!
Sincerely, Declan and Wren

Chapter 1

Wren Wilson

I've always thought my life would make a decent sitcom. Not the kind that wins awards, mind you, but one of those guilty pleasures shows you binge-watch when you're home, sick with a box of tissues and questionable judgment.

I wrangle old people for a living. Technically, my business card says, "Home Health Aide," but that doesn't quite capture the reality of what I do. I'm part nurse, part therapist, part drill sergeant, and occasionally—when Mr. Peterson decides his walker is "for sissies"—part human shield between fragile hip bones and unforgiving hardwood floors.

Today, I'm at Sunset Pines Assisted Living, where I have five regular clients. Most days I love my job. Other days... well, let's just say I understand why some animal mothers eat their young.

"Miss Wilson!" Mrs. Abernathy calls from her room as I waddle past, my scrubs clinging to my curves like they're hanging on for dear life. "You're looking pleasantly plump today!"

I pause, counting to three in my head. Mrs. Abernathy has zero filter and the observational skills of a hawk when it comes to my weight fluctuations.

"Why thank you, Mrs. A. and you're looking pleasantly ancient, as always," I reply with a sugary smile.

She cackles, delighted by our verbal sparring. "That's why you're my favorite, dear. Now come help me find my teeth. I think Gladys from 3B stole them again."

I sigh, tugging my scrub top down, over what my coworker lovingly calls our 'muffin situations'. "Your teeth are in the same place they always are—soaking in that cup by your bed."

"Oh! Well, what do you know?" She grins toothlessly.

This is my life. Hunting for dentures, distributing medications, and pretending not to notice when Mr. Gonzalez flashes me because he "forgot" to tie his bathrobe. Again.

I make my way to the nurse's station, my thighs doing that annoying rubbing thing they do when it's humid. Chub rub is real, people, and it's the bane of my existence.

"Morning, Wren," says Nurse Jackie, not looking up from her charts. "Mr. Hoffman is refusing his meds again unless, and I quote, 'that curvy girl with the smart mouth' gives them to him."

I roll my eyes so hard I nearly see my own brain.

"That old goat just likes to watch my ass when I walk away."

"Can you blame him? It's quite the view," comes a deep voice from behind me.

I freeze, feeling heat crawl up my neck. That is definitely not one of my elderly charges. That voice belongs to someone young. Male. And judging by the tingles shooting up my spine, it belongs to someone who should be illegal before noon.

I turn around and nearly swallow my tongue. Standing before me is six-plus feet of broad-shouldered, dark-haired devastation in an expensive-looking suit. His jawline could cut glass, and his eyes —the color of bourbon—are currently traveling down my body like he's memorizing the topography.

"Can I help you?" I manage, crossing my arms over my chest defensively.

He smiles, a slow, deliberate thing that does uncomfortable things to my insides. "I hope so. I'm looking for my father. He came to visit an old friend here, but he's not answering his phone."

"We don't generally let random people wander around looking for 'fathers' without more information," I say, using air quotes. "Name? Room number? Proof you're not here to steal someone's social security check?"

His eyebrows rise slightly, amusement playing at the corners of his mouth. "You're thorough. I like that."

"I'm efficient," I correct. "And you're avoiding my questions."

He takes a step closer, and I catch a whiff of something expensive and woodsy. "My father is Tomas. His friend is in room 214. Bernard Klein."

"Oh, Bernie!" I relax slightly. "He's one of mine. But visiting hours don't start for another thirty minutes."

"I'm not here to visit Bernie. I need to find my father before he—" He cuts himself off, running a hand through his hair. "It's complicated."

"Isn't it always?" I sigh, already knowing I'm going to help this ridiculously attractive man. "Fine. I'll help you look, but you stick with me. No wandering off."

"Yes, ma'am," he says with a mock salute that shouldn't be sexy but somehow is.

As we start walking down the hallway, I feel his eyes on my backside. I don't know whether to be flattered or irritated.

"So," I say over my shoulder, "you got a name, or should I just call you 'Hot Guy Looking for Dad'?"

He chuckles but doesn't answer, which is... weird.

We pass Mrs. Abernathy's open door, and she wheels herself into the doorway with impressive speed for a ninety-year-old.

"Well, well, well," she cackles, looking between us with gleeful mischief. "Wren, honey, you didn't tell me you had a gentleman caller! And such a handsome one, too. Look at how he's eyeing your backside like it's the last slice of chocolate cake!"

I want to die. Right here. Just spontaneously combust into a pile of mortified ash.

"Mrs. Abernathy," I hiss, "this is not appropriate conversation for—"

"Oh, hush," she waves dismissively. "At my age, I'm entitled to speak my mind. Young man, are you single? Our Wren here is quite a catch, you know. Curvy in all the right places, smart as a whip, and she can lift a grown man out of a bathtub without breaking a sweat."

"Mrs. A!" I sputter, my face burning hotter than the center of the sun.

The stranger's lips twitch with barely contained amusement. "Is that so?" he asks, directing the question to Mrs. Abernathy while his eyes remain fixed on me.

"Oh yes! Just last week she had to—"

"Okay!" I clap my hands together. "We really need to get going. Your teeth are in your cup, Mrs. Abernathy. Have a lovely morning!"

I practically push Mr. Mystery Man past her doorway, hearing her cackle fade behind us.

"So, you're strong enough to lift a grown man, huh?" he asks, and I swear there's a hint of admiration in his voice.

"Part of the job description," I mutter. "And you still haven't told me your name."

He stops walking suddenly, turning to face me with an intensity that makes my breath catch. "Declan.

Declan MacGallan."

The name hits me like a bucket of ice water. MacGallan. As in MacGallan Family. As in THE MacGallan Family that owns half the city and is rumored to have connections that make the local police suddenly develop amnesia whenever their name comes up.

"You're..." I swallow hard, taking an instinctive step back.

"Yes." His eyes narrow slightly, watching my reaction carefully. "Is that going to be a problem?"

Before I can answer, a commotion erupts from the common room down the hall. I hear Bernie's distinctive voice raised in anger, followed by another man's shouts.

"Shit," Declan mutters, already moving toward the noise.

I hurry after him, professionalism kicking in, despite my sudden realization that I'm dealing with actual Irish mafia royalty. When we reach the common room, the scene is chaos. Bernie is standing, pointing a shaky finger at a distinguished older man who must be Tomas MacGallan. Three other elderly residents are watching with the rapt attention of people who haven't had this much excitement since the cafeteria served wine with dinner on Christmas.

"You think you can just walk in here and threaten me?" Bernie shouts, his thin voice cracking. "After all these years, you still think you own me?"

"Dad," Declan says sharply, striding into the room.

Tomas MacGallan turns, and the family resemblance is unmistakable—same cutting jawline, same intimidating presence, though time has softened his edges.

"Declan. I told you to wait in the car," Tomas says, his accent thicker than his son's.

"Clearly that would have been a mistake," Declan responded, rolling his eyes.

"Declan," his father says again, voice dropping to a dangerous octave. "Outside. Now."

I step forward, instinct kicking in. "Actually, Mr. MacGallan, I need to ask everyone to lower their voices. This is a care facility, not a boxing ring."

Both MacGallan men turn to look at me like I've grown a second head. Clearly, these aren't men used to being told what to do.

"And who might you be?" Tomas asks, his accent curling around the words.

"I'm Wren Wilson, Bernie's home health aide." I straighten my spine, trying to appear more authoritative than I feel in my faded scrubs. "And whatever business you have with him needs to happen at a reasonable volume or not at all."

Bernie's trembling hand finds my arm. "It's alright, Wren. Old business. Nothing for you to worry about."

"Doesn't sound like nothing," I mutter, eyeing the elder MacGallan suspiciously.

Declan steps closer, placing himself between his father and us. "Dad, you promised this would be civil."

"It was until he threatened to—"

"I never threatened anything!" Bernie protests. "I just said I was thinking about writing my memoirs!"

Oh. Well, that explains a lot.

"Gentlemen," I interject firmly. "Whatever this is about, it needs to be handled elsewhere. Mr. Klein's blood pressure medication doesn't allow for this kind of excitement."

Tomas MacGallan studies me for a long moment before his weathered face cracks into an unexpected smile. "You've got spine, girl. Not many people would step between me and... old friends."

"Part of the job," I reply, not backing down.

"Dad," Declan says quietly. "Let's go. We can discuss this later."

The older man nods curtly. "Bernard, think carefully about what I said. Some stories are better left untold."

With that cryptic warning, he turns and walks out with the dignity of a king, leaving an uncomfortable silence in his wake.

"Well," I said after a moment. "That was dramatic."

Bernie sinks back into his chair, suddenly looking every one of his eighty-plus years. "Sorry about that, Wren. Old ghosts."

"You okay?" I ask, kneeling beside him to check his

pulse. A bit rapid, but nothing alarming.

"Fine, fine." He waves me off. "Known that stubborn ass since we were kids. He always did have a flair for the dramatic."

I feel Declan watching us, his expression unreadable. When I look up, our eyes lock, and something electric passes between us.

"I should go," he says, though he makes no move to leave.

"Probably," I agree, also not moving.

Bernie looks between us and snorts. "For God's sake, just ask for her number and be done with it."

Chapter 2

A year later

Declan MacGallan

The road to Pearl Lake stretches before me like a winding confession, each curve revealing another slice of countryside I couldn't care less about. My hands grip the steering wheel of the Cadillac Escalade V tighter than necessary, the leather creaking under my fingers. Six months of searching, and finally, a lead that doesn't end in a dead end or a body. It all came in the form of a text message. Ironically, from a high school buddy of mine who just happened to have fallen in love with my cousin.

"You're grinding your teeth again," Rory says from the passenger seat, not looking up from his tablet. "Your dentist is going to charge extra for that."

"Fuck my dentist," I mutter, easing off the gas as we approach the village limits. "And fuck Luke for making me come all the way out to butt fuck nowhere instead of just telling me what he knows over the phone."

Rory snorts. "Maybe Luke doesn't trust phones?"

I don't ask. With Luke, it's better not to know the details.

Two black SUVs follow behind us, carrying the rest of my team— the Reapers, the killers of the clan. Overkill for a simple information exchange, maybe, but nothing about Brit's disappearance has been simple.

My cousin. My responsibility. My failure.

The GPS chirps, directing me to turn onto a gravel road that leads to a Victorian inn overlooking the lake. Luke's text said to meet him here at his aunt Kim's inn.

"Place looks dead," Rory observes as we pull into the empty parking lot.

I park and kill the engine, scanning the surroundings with practiced precision. "He better be here."

We exit the SUV, and the other vehicles pull in behind us. Four men emerge—Vince, Torres, Maddox, and Keller, each one scanning different sections of the perimeter.

"Keep it casual," I order, as I send Luke a text telling him we arrived. "We're not here to start a war."

My phone pings and I look at the text from Luke telling me to go around the back, to the restaurant.

I look at Rory. "Take them and head inside, get registered. Reservation for four rooms. I'm heading around to the back."

Rory nods as I walk away, headed for the restaurant.

I walk in and see him sitting there. He stood up the second he saw me, motioning me to join him. We meet in a bear hug, and for a minute it feels like it hasn't been 15 years since we last saw one another.

"Declan, it's been a few years, hasn't it?" he grins, gesturing to the seat across the table.

"It certainly has. What happened to the skinny ass nerd that played video games all day?" I laughed.

"Well, I still play video games, but now I do it for a living, and I just blossomed into the magnificent physique that's before you," he chuckled. "You're not too shabby looking yourself, Declan, what happened to you?"

I could feel the dark look cross my face before it disappeared, replaced by the carefree, friendly grin that he remembered. "The family business, speaking of which"— I look around — "where is that dear cousin of mine?"

I leaned back in my chair as a waitress came over to the table and set a glass of water in front of us. Luke looked up at her and said, "We will need one more, Jasmine, Brit will be joining us shortly."

"Alright, will you guys be having the buffet, or do you want menus?" she asked.

"Buffet," we said in unison.

"Okay, help yourself whenever you're ready, I'll be back with more water."

I looked at him. "So how long is Brit going to be because my stomach is about to eat itself."

"Mine too. And who knows, Kim needed her to try something on, and you know how women are when it comes to clothes." He stood up. "C'mon, let's grab a plate before it's all gone."

We made our way over to the table and each took a plate, starting to pile it high with food. Taking a scoop of scalloped potatoes, I plopped it onto my plate. "So, have you told her why I'm here?"

He made a face. "She doesn't know you're here at all."

"What?" I asked in disbelief. "How could you not tell her? If she sees me before knowing the reason I'm here, she's going to run."

And run she did.

Right into the very arms of the guy who had brought her to Pearl Lake. The one that was supposed to be in jail for kidnapping her.

"Would it kill you to offer clearer directions next time?" I asked Luke as I got out of the SUV, a mile away from the old emu farm she ran to. "Seen any signs of life yet?"

"Nothing so far," he replied, his breath misting in the cold air. "No shadows or movement from inside."

"Alright, my crew will take the outbuildings," I decided, studying him with a hint of concern. "You sure you're up to going in the house alone, or do you want company?"

"With this, I'll be fine," Luke answered, waving a tire iron.

I clucked my tongue. "Seriously? Planning to hurl that at him, are you? Rory," I called out. He promptly handed me a handgun. "Here, better to be armed than sorry." I held it out to him.

Luke flinched slightly. "I'm not sure about using that."

"Just take it," I persisted, pressing the gun into his hand. "Safety's off. Just remember, finger away from the trigger unless you're ready to fire. You've shot a gun before, haven't you?"

"A BB gun," he declared with a nod.

I let out a laugh. "Ever hit your mark?"

"Every time." He just failed to tell me at the time it was the side of a barn.

"That'll do then," I said. I spun around to address the men. "Chris, you're on watch. Eyes peeled on the house and out for any police — wouldn't put it past your aunt to have them on speed dial. Let's move," I motioned to the others.

We stealthily made our way through the trees and into the yard. We dispersed like a swat team once we approached the property. Once every building was cleared, we headed into the house.

With my men at my back, I stood in the doorway of the bedroom, scanning the room. Her captor, I presume, was out cold, laying on the floor. Luke was sitting on the bed, in the process of removing the binds at Brit's wrists where she was tied to the post on the headboard. The second they were off she flung herself into his arms, sobbing.

"So, you didn't have to use the gun after all?" I chuckled from the doorway.

Luke looked up at me and grinned. "Didn't even use the tire iron. I put him in a chokehold."

"Wow, I'm impressed," I nodded. Moving into the room to look down at the man sprawled there and nudged his leg with the toe of my boot. "Boys, clean this mess up," I ordered my men as I took a seat on the edge of the bed.

Brit must have remembered what Luke did to betray her trust, she pulled away from him and got up to stand by the window. She looked at us, sitting side by side on the bed. Giving Luke the evil eye, she must have decided she would deal with him later, but for now, she was going to deal with me. I could tell by the look in her eye as she raised her chin.

"So, you found me huh? Now what? I suppose you're planning on taking me back to Toronto?"—she folded her arms across her chest— "I'm letting you know I'm not going."

I looked at Luke and sighed. "I told you; you should have told her."

"Yeah, I know you did. You saw the look she sent me,"— Luke shot a hand in her direction— "if I had, she would be laying sprawled out on the floor."

Brit couldn't believe what she was hearing. The two of us bickering back and forth like two old ladies.

She stamped her foot to get our attention. "I am here, you know!"

I gave her a bored look, while Luke grinned at her.

"So you are," I yawned standing and moved towards her. "My dear cousin. If you hadn't taken off running and had dined with us at lunch, you would have discovered that it wasn't my dad searching for you, it was me."

"What?! There were missing persons posters looking for me. I saw it with my own eyes… with a reward!"

I put an arm around her shoulders and waved my hand about in the air. "Yeah, well that was just for show. I would never have paid it."

Luke laughed like he was on the intel of an inside joke. "I would pay it Brit," he said with a wink.

"Yeah, well that's because you're an idiot. No woman is worth fifty grand."

Chapter 3

Wren

"How could you fucking do this to me dad?"

"Wren, I'm sorry. I had no choice; they were going to kill me."

"That's fine. Just so you know, you have been dead to me for years."

Those words ring in my ears as I stand in a wedding dress in front of the full-length mirror, looking at my reflection. Harsh, I know, but when I had asked my father that question a month ago, tears were streaming from my eyes. He had just told me that I was getting married.

Funny, but I didn't have a man in my life, other than him, nor did I want one. I was happy being single. Taking care of my elderly patients was my only mission in life. One that I would happily do until my retirement in thirty five years.

But here I stand. In a little church, God knows where, as I was blindfolded the whole trip, awaiting my fate because my father decided to gamble his life savings away. Borrowing money from a loan shark was his fault, not mine. But I was the one that was going to pay off his debt, with my life, by marrying the shark's son. A union that neither of us want.

I turn away from the mirror and eye the narrow lone window. It beckons me, and I make my way over to it and glance out into the dark night. Cupping my hands around my eyes, I press my nose against the windowpane and see nothing but trees. Good. There's at least cover for me to escape into. I reach for the lock and shove the sash up. I'm excited to find that it glides smoothly without a sound but stops after six inches. Raising my eyes to the frame, I glare at the nail coated in paint that was hammered into the wood.

"Damnit!"

Breaking the window would only attract unwanted attention. Even if I wanted to chance it, looking at the width of the frame, there was no way I'd fit through it. If I were twenty pounds lighter, maybe.

Echoing footsteps on the other side of the door had me closing it just as it burst open.

A burly man stood there, the gun at his waist did not go unnoticed by me. "Come on, it's time."

I walk across the room, and he steps aside to let me pass.

I step into the hall as the sound of the wedding march begins over the church's sound system. Unsure of which way leads to my doom, I ask, "Where do I go?"

"Left."

We make our way down the hall to the nave, and I feel a bubble of laughter start in my chest. It's either laughing my ass off or crying at the absurdity of it all. But I suppress it. As I pass each pew, I notice the wilted flowers from a long-ago wedding adorn each one of them. This little church was once a place of happiness, but now it's filled with my anxiety as it leaches out of my pores.

I raise my eyes to my 'groom'. The look he casts my way says it all. I was wrong when I thought he was just as reluctant as I am. He looks like a lecher as his eyes devour me, and I know in my heart he will treat me like an unloved dog. That is not going to happen.

My body simply refusing to go another step further, I stop at the last pew and survey my surroundings. The preacher is standing there with the Holy book in his hands, a look of sadness upon his face. Behind my soon to be hubby, stands, what I can only assume is his best man and behind him another man with a bulge under his suit jacket. That tells me he's just another henchman like the one standing at my back.

"Where is everyone?" I ask. I need to know what I'm dealing with before I act.

"This is it," comes the squeaky response from my groom's lips. Lips that look like earthworms.

If I was unsure of following through with what I was about to do, his voice and those soil dwelling, lookalike worms that rimmed his mouth, sealed the deal.

I shudder at the thought of him pressing them onto me, anywhere. "I don't even know your name."

He grinned at me. "You'll know soon enough"— he reached out his hand to me— "Preacher, you may start."

I don't take his hand, but I do move to stand beside him. It's the only way that I can get close enough to the candle that is standing on a dais beside the preacher. Its heavy holder is my weapon of choice. It's my only weapon, and one that I need to get closer to. I turn and look at my groom. "Can I ask the preacher something, in private?"

He shakes his head. "Not in private, but you may go up to him and whisper it in his ear." He grins at me again, and I can just imagine what he's thinking. Thinking I have a special request for our nuptials.

I smile at him, I mean it's a small token of thanks, the only one that I will offer to him and then glance over my shoulder. The man that escorted me here is standing to my right. Perfect.

As demurely as I can, I gather my skirts in my hands and take a step up beside the preacher. He leans down as I lean forward. Our bodies conceal my left hand as I grab hold of the candle. Softly, I whisper into his ear. "Duck."

The man drops like a sack of potatoes as I swing around. With wax dripping down my arm, I take aim right at my intended and conk him on the head. Blood starts to pour from the gash on his forehead at the same time as he backhands me across the face. My head whips back from the force, but I stand my ground. And when I turn back to look at him, instead of the guns I'm expecting to see in my face, he's laying on the floor spasming. I'm forgotten as chaos ensues, and his henchmen hurry to his side.

That's my cue.

"Chubby legs don't fail me now," I mutter to myself as I gather my skirts high. My heels go flying as I kick them off and run down the aisle. I don't look back as I fling the doors open and the reassuring sound of them banging closed urges me on at a full tilt. I run blindly into the snowy night, my breath hitching in my throat, my chest on fire. I have no idea where I'm headed, I just know I need to get the hell away from the little church as fast as possible.

A set of headlights weaving through the barren trees becomes my beacon. It tells me that a road is nearby. Halfway there, I slip on an icy patch, my feet flying out from under me, I fall with a thud. The wind is knocked out of me momentarily. I'm dazed and gasping for a lungful of air that freezes in my throat. In a way, it was a good thing I suppose, because it allowed me to hear the thundering footsteps crashing through the undergrowth. The henchmen are coming.

I'm thankful for the snowy white gown I'm wearing. It conceals me as they pass by in long strides, and I can suck in the frigid air that my lungs crave when they do. I count to ten before I scramble to my feet and start running in the opposite direction of them.

I run through the trees, cursing like a sailor as a tree limb just about takes me out, and I stumble onto a path. It's a narrow one, but from what I can tell, it leads due south, right towards the headlights I had seen.

"There she is!" I hear one of the goons call out.

Ducking down is out of the question, they will be on me in a matter of seconds if I do. Instead, I yank my skirts up and take off down the sloping ground towards anything but them.

"I got her!" One of them shouts, and I swear I can feel his breath on my neck. With one last oomph, I break through the trees and land face first on to the lonely snow-covered road. With the blood rushing through my veins and pounding in my ears, I lay there, still as a stone catching my breath. The road is no longer lonely. A car is coming right at me, and I would rather it finish me off than what's to come if they get their hands on me. Squeezing my eyes shut, I pray that it will be quick and relatively painless. That was until I heard it sliding to a stop and a car door slamming.

I cringe at the expletive coming from a man with such a deep velvety voice. If he hadn't just said what he did, I might have melted in my underwear. I feel his strong hands turn me over, and my eyes meet his for a fleeting second before they roam over my body.

He lifts my shoulders off the road and aims my face towards the car's LED headlights. I look directly in his eyes. How I saw them darken, with the lights glaring in mine is beyond me. But when he sees the black eye and fat lip that I'm currently sporting, thanks to my intended, that's exactly what happened. Or maybe it wasn't that I saw them darken but rather felt the heat flashing from those bourbon-colored eyes.

Chapter 4

Declan

I'm in no hurry as I leave from the shores of Pearl Lake on my own. Rory and the others returned the previous day, and I savor the solitude.

I set the cruise on the Caddy at a pace reminiscent of the Sunday drives that I grew up with as a kid. Why? Because I don't look forward to the drive back to Toronto. Truth be told, I would rather have stayed in the lakeside village getting to know Brit a bit better while shooting the shit with Luke. The guilt still eats at me, the way my father treated her. Making her work as a call girl just so her mother could get the medical attention she needed. Worst part was, long after the debt had been paid, he never told her. He just let her keep raking in the money for the 'family'.

But I can't. Not when that same family is waiting back in Toronto for my return. I use that term loosely. The only blood family that I have waiting for me is my father, the 'Captain', whom half the time doesn't even remember me. Now, well into his seventies and sadly living in the past, I'm heading back not as his son but as his replacement. Officially. Once I have my swearing in ceremony, that is. It's a job that I've been doing for the past six months. One that I don't want.

Being the most powerful family in Toronto has its advantages. The MacGallan's are known for putting the fear in many, without the need of too much force, and the cops always look the other way. But sometimes we need to show those who want to take over our city, who is boss. A job that I enjoyed and didn't mind doing in my younger days when my father became Captain. Now at 35, I'm the second in command, and I miss the hands-on contact that I had over our enemies. Now, I dole out the orders to the others. The reapers are the ones who take care of the dirty jobs. Just like the one we had done in Pearl Lake. Taking care of the man that had abducted Brit and kept her for over a month, was something I would have gladly taken care of myself. But that job had fallen to them. The captain to be, could no longer soil his hands in such a fashion. Fuck. I would give my left testicle to be involved in that part of the business again.

The snow is starting to come down heavier, and I flick the windshield wipers on. For the next mile or so, they begin to freeze up, and I have no choice but to pull off to the side of the road. Shifting the SUV into park, I reach behind the passenger seat and get the snowbrush. Scowling, I shove my door open and make my way around it to start clearing the windshield.

I make one swipe when I hear a call coming

through the Caddy's speakers and glance at my watch. It's Connor, the only man that I trust in the 'family' to leave my father alone with.

I lay the brush down on the SUV's hood and bite a gloved finger. Pulling my hand out of it, I tap my watch and accept the call. "Talk to me man."

"Declan... I'm sorry, your dad—"

Cursing the snow, I slip the glove back on and pick up the brush as I snap out, "What about him?"

"...He's gone."

My hand freezes mid swipe. "What did you just say?"

"He took off. He was sitting at the table while I was cooking dinner. I turned around to ask him if he wanted an extra baked potato, you know how he likes—"

"What do you mean he took off?"

"That's what I'm trying to tell you."

Through gritted teeth I spit out, "Then stop talking about fucking potatoes and get to the point!"

Connor swallows so hard that I can hear him through the speakers. "Right, sorry. I turned around, and he was gone. I searched the whole house from top to bottom. It's like he just disappeared."

Moving around the driver's door, I toss the snowbrush into the backseat, climb behind the wheel, and throw the gear shift into drive. "How long ago was this? Did you check to see if any of the car keys are missing?"

"Twenty minutes," Connor mumbled. "And no, I didn't think to check for the keys."

"Call the others and tell them to get to the house. In the meantime, go check the garage, see if he's in there or if any cars are missing." I glance at the screen of the GPS and press my foot down on the accelerator despite the snow. "I'm an hour out. With this weather it's looking closer to an hour and a half. Find my fucking father Connor, or you're a dead man. And tell the rest of the men, they're dead too if he's not found."

"Yes sir. I'll call you the second we find him."

"You do that." I disconnect the call and start to drive as fast as the weather allows me to.

"Fuck!!!" I hit the steering wheel in frustration. My mind starts to drift off to the what if's. What if he's just in a closet, unable to find his way out. Or What if he's laying in a snowdrift freezing to death. The head of our clan was always a ruthless son of a bitch. Didn't care about anyone, not even his own son, but for the life of me, I can't feel hatred towards him. God knows I tried. But that man is no longer my father. My father is now an old and feeble man reliving his childhood, where he was happiest. Maybe losing his memory is a good thing, he won't remember how much blood is on his hands when he goes to meet his maker.

Knowing I can't do a damn thing about what's going on at home, I turn on my Spotify playlist for a distraction from my thoughts. I start thumbing the forward button on the steering wheel as I glance at the screen looking for that perfect song. Judgement Day by Five Finger Death Punch fits the bill, and I look back to the road, settling in for the long ride.

If it had taken me a second longer, I would have missed the object flying out of the forest along the side of the road. It landed right in my path, fifty feet in front of me, and didn't move. Slamming on the brakes, I feel the tires trying desperately to gain purchase in the snow, I crank the wheel into the oncoming lane. Thanks to the mound of snow between it and mine, the SUV comes to a stop. I park it right there and shove my door open and get out. I slam it shut so hard that I'm half expecting to hear the telltale sound of glass cracking. I'm glad it doesn't, that would make for a very cold ride back to home.

"Cock. *Sucker!*"

I need this delay like I need a gun pointed at my head. Rounding the front of the SUV, I stalk over to the thing and discover it's a woman, in a wedding dress of all things. Glancing around, I see nothing but trees and wonder why the hell she flew out of the forest like she was a bad meal being regurgitated.

I kneel beside her and take hold of her shoulders, turning her over. A mop of wheat colored hair falls from the bun on her head, covering her face, and I brush it aside. Our eyes meet, and I'm momentarily stunned at the clarity of those green eyes looking so fearfully in mine and yet I feel I've seen them before. I force myself to look away, checking for any signs of blood stains on her gown. Her ample breasts are threatening to pop out over the low neckline of the gown, but I ignore them. When I see no blood, I look back in those eyes. Eyes that I could easily drown in. And that's when I see the dark circle just above her cheek. She has a black eye, I'm sure of it. Lifting her shoulders off the ground, I angle her towards the headlights of the Cadillac. I feel a rage settle in the pit of my stomach. Not only does she have a black eye, but she also has a bloody fat lip.

"Lady, who the fuck did this to you on your wedding day?"

Before she can answer, a rustling sound comes from the tree line, and I look to see two figures standing there. In hushed tones they talk amongst themselves, and I can hear my name whispered.

The woman looks at me and visibly cowers. Apparently, she did too and knows who I am.

Before either of us can say a thing, a voice calls out. "MacGallan. Just leave her there and be on your way. The boss won't like it if you interfere."

I almost laughed at that. The guy had balls to tell me what to do. There was no way I was leaving her there.

"Get up," I murmured. She looked like she was contemplating which would be the worse of the two evils, me or the men that had been chasing her. Finally, when she placed her hand in mine, it felt like I was holding ice. I took my coat off and draped it around her shoulders before guiding her to the passenger side of the Caddy. Pulling on the handle, I held the door open and helped her onto the seat.

I cranked up the heat and turned on the heated seat for her before I closed the door and started walking around to the driver's side.

"MacGallan," the voice called out again. "If you take her, you're going to have a war on your hands."

That was music to my ears. Stopping, I looked towards the forest and just before climbing behind the wheel, I said, "Tell your boss to bring it on."

"Don't you want to know who he is?"

"Did I ask who he was? No. I said, bring it on."

Closing my door, I looked over to where she was sitting. Her eyes were fixed on her lap.

"You have your seatbelt on?" I ask.

A slight nod of her head was the only indication that she heard me.

Chapter 5

Wren

As the lights of an approaching town come into view, I sit in the passenger seat, stunned while what I did back in the church sinks in. I'm the type of person that will catch a house fly and let it outside. How can I be a killer? I start to shiver uncontrollably as the shock takes over, and Declan must think I'm just cold because he turns the temperature of the heater up to 80° F. He doesn't remember me, but I do remember him. The day he walked into the Sunset Pines looking for his father. His eyes and that velvety voice of his haunted me for months afterwards.

"Where are your shoes?" he asks.

I swallow the lump in my throat before I look at him and mumble, "I kicked them off in the church."

A smile tugs at the corner of his mouth. "Of course. Doesn't everyone?"

I bite my bottom lip to stop it trembling when he glances at me. "I hit him on the forehead with a candlestick." My mind screams at me to shut up, that I'm confessing to murder, but I can't, not when he looks at me a second time. "I killed him."

He scratches his head and takes a deep breath. "What makes you say that?"

I open my mouth to answer but nothing comes out. The image of my intended flopping around on the floor in a pool of his own blood plays through my mind.

Placing his hand on my knee, he gives it a gentle squeeze, bringing me back to the present. "What makes you say that?" he repeats.

"Th... there was just so much blood, and he fell to the floor after he hit me... laying there... his body was jerking."

He put his hand back on the steering wheel as we approached the outskirts of the town. I let my head loll back against the seat as I stare out my window seeing a sign on the side of the road welcoming us to the village Brechin.

"If he hit you with enough force to give you that black eye and fat lip, he's not dead. Trust me. Head wounds are especially bloody."

I lean forward and look at him with hope filled eyes. "Are you certain?"

He stops the car at a red light, what looks to be the only traffic light in the village and turns towards me. "Yeah, I'm certain."

A flash of red and blue lights from behind light up the interior of the vehicle, and I tense in my seat.

Declan looks in his driver's side mirror at the police

officer as he gets out of his car and starts to lower his window. "Relax. He isn't here for you."

I sit there staring straight ahead as the cop stops to stand by the car and leans down to look inside. "Evening folks, where are you headed?"

"Making our way back home to Toronto," Declan says.

"Nasty night to be doing that." The cop stands straight and points to the road ahead. "You won't be able to head that way. Road's closed in both directions about a mile or so out of town, snowplough is in the ditch."

Declan looks past me down the street and asks, "What about that way? Where does it head to?"

"Lagoon City and Lake Simcoe," the cop replies.

Declan jerked his thumb to the left. "And that way?"

"A quarry."

Declan pursed his lips. "Right. So, what you're saying is we're stuck here?"

"Yep. There's a Wild Wing up the road ahead. Owners live nearby and opened for those stranded. If you want, I can escort you there, or you can pick an empty parking lot to bunk down for the night."

Declan turned to me. "Are you hungry?"

I shrug. "I could eat something. But I would love to use the bathroom."

He looked back at the officer and said, "Wild Wing

it is."

As the cop makes his way back to his patrol car, Declan puts up his window. "The second they open the road, we're leaving."

It's not like I wanted to camp out in a restaurant. I nod my agreement, and we set off crawling behind the police car. I grab the 'oh shit bar' as the Caddy starts to fishtail, but I don't say a word. A quick glance at him tells me he's enjoying my discomfort from the grin on his face.

"You're safe," he murmurs, and he says it in a way that causes my blood to hum in my veins. Which terrifies me even more. He's a killer for cripe's sake. How can I be attracted to that? But then I remember, despite what he says, so am I.

"Before we go inside, I'll get you some clothes from my bag. You can change in the back seat."

"Okay. Thank you."

He turns on the signal light, and we follow the cop as he pulls into the parking lot of the restaurant. We stop as the officer goes wide then circles back and pulls up beside the SUV. Declan rolls down the window, and the two begin to exchange a few words.

I squeeze my thighs tight, half listening because I'm trying so hard to not empty my bladder on his leather seat. But then I hear something that I can't ignore.

"We don't want any trouble here Mr. MacGallan. Once the road opens, be on your way."

"That's the plan, officer," Declan says. "Drive safe."

Declan doesn't move the SUV until the cop pulls back onto the road and heads back to the village.

"Your reputation precedes you. How did he know your name?" I ask as he parks closer to the building.

"He ran my plate back at the traffic light," he said, taking off his seat belt. Reaching into the back seat, he dragged a bag onto his lap and unzipped it. Pulling out a pair of track pants and a pullover sweater, he handed them to me.

"Here, put these on your feet." He tossed a pair of socks on top of the clothes.

"I don't have any shoes."

"I'll carry you inside." He jerked his head towards the back seat, then picked up his phone. "Get in the back and change."

Flustered at the thought of being in his arms, I sputtered. "Y... you can't carry me!"

"Of course, I can." He looked up from his phone and stared me in the face. "What are you, 145 pounds wet?"

I snort. If he wanted to think I only weighed 145, who was I to tell him differently? "No, you cannot!"

He looked back down at his phone. "We'll see. Now get in the back and change. I need to make a call."

I undid my seatbelt and gathered the skirt of the gown. "You're not carrying me," I mumbled as I squeezed myself between the seats.

I collapsed face first onto the leather and pushed myself up. How the skirt got from my hand to covering my head was beyond me, but here I was. Half into the back seat with my panty clad ass bare for him to see.

Flailing my legs about, I felt my shin contact something solid, it was his head. I know because he growled. "Woman, what the hell are you doing?"

"A little help would be great," came my muffled reply.

His hot hands on my chilled skin were a soothing balm that I didn't know I needed. As he shoved my legs into the backseat a calming came over me that is unexplainable considering my circumstances.

I righted myself on the seat and glanced towards him. He was staring at me with an odd, fierce look on his face.

I gulped. "What?"

"Are you good now?"

"Peachy."— I motioned with my hand— "You can turn around now."

He raised a brow. "Oh, can I? What if I would rather watch, Miss… I don't even know your name."

"It's Wren." I answered as a few thoughts entered my head. Why? Why would he want to watch me, a short frumpy hot mess of a woman and did that mean he was attracted to me? Because if it did, I'm not sure I wanted that kind of attention from him. Yes, he was hot and sexy and had a glorious voice that turned my bones to mush. And because of all that, he had to have a woman waiting for him at home. I decided he was testing me, and there was no right or wrong answer. "We've met."

He looked at me, his eyes studying my face in the light from the dashboard. Recognition flared in his. "Sunset Pines."

Without a word, I crossed my arms over my chest and fixed my gaze on him. I could do that all night. As a kid I was the champion starer in my neighborhood, and right now, I knew I couldn't back down. If I did, it showed a sign of weakness, something he probably got off on. I was relieved when the sound of an incoming call interrupted our staring contest.

Chapter 6

Declan

Ah right! The woman who can lift a grown man out of a bathtub. She reminds me more of a Canada Goose, than the fragile bird she's named after.

"Connor. You better tell me you found him." I say it in a way of greeting.

"We found him. He was hiding in a closet on the third floor. Apparently, he wanted to play hide and seek."

Thankful, I let out a sigh of relief. I really hadn't wanted to kill Connor.

"Good. Police have the road closed off, and we won't be home for a while. Possibly tomorrow."

"We, sir?"

"Yeah. There will be a…"—My eyes dart to the rear-view mirror as the vehicle rocks under her movements, and I catch a flash of a silky white bra on its surface— "…guest arriving with me. Ready the room in the east wing for her."

"Absolutely. Shall I tell the other men that you no

longer will be hunting them down now that your father is safe?"

I wince at the question. Not that I never meant it, I'd just rather Wren didn't know that I was willing to kill my own men. "Yeah, tell them. Also, get Rory to look… hang on a second."

A thought just occurred to me. Leaning my head back against the seat I turned my head and said, "Little goose, where are you from?"

"Did you just call me a goose?!"

I chuckled at the slip of my tongue, and the emphasis of how she said the word. "Yeah. Where are you from?"

She stuck her face between the seats, and her body soon followed. Settling herself in the passenger seat, she blew a stray hair out of her face— "Etobicoke."— and proceeded to put on the socks.

I swallowed hard. This wasn't the same woman who had flopped into my backseat a few minutes ago. Her hair was pulled free from the bun she had been sporting, and it laid in a gentle wave past her shoulders, softly framing her face.

I look away because the sight of her wearing my clothes has my dick springing to attention.

I bark into the phone. "Get Rory to check out loan sharks that are trying to branch out in Etobicoke and any surrounding suburbs of ours for that matter, ASAP."

Connor laughed. "You're joking, right? Who would

be so dumb to even try?"

"That's what I need to find out."

"Okay sir. I'll tell him to report any findings to you directly."

"You do that. And Connor, don't lose my father again, or next time I'll cut your bal—" I could feel her eyes on me. "... balance of your weekly paycheck."

I disconnected the call and glanced at her and watched as her lips pulled in a smirk. I want to smack my own on them, wiping it off her face.

I don't let on though. She can't know the effect she has on me. I look out my window and clear my throat. "Are you ready?" I ask. The telltale rasp of my voice betraying that I'm aroused has me inwardly cursing, and I shove my door open.

Instead of her taking my cue of leaving the vehicle, she sat there with wide eyes. "How did you know about the loan shark?"

With one foot on the ground and my ass half on the seat, I look out the windshield and sigh. It's not like it was any of her business, but from the looks of stance, she wasn't going anywhere until I answered her. "Because one of those men back there used to work for me. I've been keeping tabs on him. Now, are you ready?"

She nods but doesn't say anything. I wonder if she's contemplating on how she's going to get inside the restaurant without getting frostbite on her toes. She needn't know that I deliberately parked far away from it.

I shut my door and walk around to her side of the SUV. She's putting the coat on, and as I open her door, she moves to slide off the seat into the snow but stops.

Her eyes flash up at mine. "I didn't realize it was so deep."

"Yeah. It is." I bend forward to pick her up, and she starts squawking.

"You're not carrying me. I'll just stay here."

"Nope, you're coming with me because you're not using my vehicle as a bathroom." I tuck my arms under her knees and lift her up effortlessly. She wraps her arms around my neck, and I kick the door closed.

"I wonder if they sell shoes inside," she mutters, as her hair whips around in the wind, and I laugh.

Spitting out a mouthful of her hair, I say, "If they do, I'll buy you a pair. Open the door, would you?"

Her arm tightens around my neck as she grabs the handle with her opposite hand, and together, we work as a team getting inside.

The second the door shut behind us, she started.

"Put me down."

I ignore her and carry her through a second set of doors that stand open and greet the man standing behind the counter.

"Hi there. You two feel free to find a spot that you're comfortable with. Would you like something warm to drink?"

"Coffee is good," I say as I make my way to an empty booth by a window and set her down on the seat.

She leans forward and hisses. "You didn't have to carry me all the way, you know."

I take a seat across from her and flip the coffee cup in front of me over. "And get your feet wet?"

She flipped her hair over her shoulder and did the same with her cup as a waitress came by with a pot of coffee.

"Hello folks. Ginny is my name." She nods towards the window as she starts to fill our cups. "Nasty night out there, isn't it?"

"That it is," I said. "It was nice of the owners to open up for those stranded."

"That would be me and the hubby, Mike, you met him at the door." She set the coffee pot on the table and said, "Kitchen is open too. We aren't doing the whole menu, but if you're wanting wings or a burger and fries, you just let me know."

Wren gripped the edge of the table. "I would love to use the bathroom. Where might that be?"

Ginny points towards the doors we came in. "Past the front counter. Head into that darkened room there and head right. There's a hallway there with a light on. Women's washroom is the first on the right."

Wren smiles and scoots off the seat. "I'll be right back."

"Goose, do you want anything to eat?"

She slowly turns her head around and looks at me over her shoulder. "I'm good, you go ahead though."

Once she was out of earshot, I looked at Ginny. "Do you have any finger foods that you can whip up?"

"Did you call her a goose?"

I chuckle as I add sugar to my coffee. "Yeah, because she has the attitude of one."

Ginny smiled. "Makes sense then. And yes, I can fix you a platter of finger foods. Be back in a few." She picked up the coffee pot and made her way towards a set of double swinging doors, filling other stranded motorist's cups as she went.

I look out the window and stare at the snow in the parking lot's light. The snow is relentless. I lean forward and look down to the path I'd made walking from the SUV. It's already filling in.

Wren is coming back with a smile on her face, and I'm mesmerized by it. If I never had another memory in my life, I would be happy with this moment etched in my mind for the rest of it.

"What did you do?" I murmur, matching her smile as she sits down.

She takes the sugar and pours a spoonful into her cup. "I didn't do anything. But they have a gift shop in that back room." She adds three little creamers to her cup and gives it a good stir.

I watch her every move, and I feel like a creep for doing it. She puckers her lips as she picks up her mug then blows onto the brew before taking a delicate sip.

"Whoa, that's hot! But soooo good." She smacks her lips together then licks them, and I want to trace that same path with my tongue.

"Show me."

She raises her brows at me. "Beg your pardon?"

I move to stand and hold my hand out to her. "Show me the gift shop."

A soft "Oh" escapes past her lips, and she takes it. And when she drops it the second she's on her feet, that's fine with me. Because she takes off in the direction of the gift shop, and I get a nice view of my track pants caressing her ass with her every step. My mind goes to her wedged between the seats in the SUV. The smooth skin of her calves was the only thing I touched, but I so wanted to smooth my hand up her thighs, to her full hips and plump bottom. I was tempted to spank it but thought better of it at the last moment.

"Here it is," she said, stopping in front of a little room with glass walls, and a sign that says 'Closed'. She presses her face against the door and cups her hands around her eyes.

"I think they have boots over there, but I can't quite make it out," she says.

When I don't answer her, she turns to look at me.

I know what she saw when she looked at me. She saw a fever burning in the depths of my eyes. One that was for her and her alone.

Chapter 7

Wren

I turn to look at him and see a ravenous look in his eyes. Wondering where that look came from, I glance around the empty room. Is there a stunning woman nearby that I hadn't seen but he did? There's no one there, and I wonder if instead he's sick, and I just misinterpreted the glaze in his eyes.

But then my eyes drop for some strange reason to the bulge in his jeans, and I realize that isn't the case. He has a hard on, and it's for me.

"Little goose," he mutters through clenched teeth. "Go back to the table. Now!"

He didn't have to tell me twice. I go to skirt around him, but his hand snakes out and grabs my wrist, holding me to the spot in a firm but gentle vise.

His voice is smooth, like velvety chocolate caressing my senses as I sink my teeth into the perfect bonbon, when he says, "I'll be a minute. Ask Ginny if those are boots in the gift shop and if they are, get a pair."

I can't speak because my heart is wedged in my throat, beating like a drum. Instead, I nod, knowing exactly why he needs to take a minute. I know, because my underwear is soaked, and I'm thankful that I'm wearing the only pair of moisture wicking panties that I own.

He lets go of my wrist, and I walk away. Halfway to the table I glance back to see him still standing there, his silhouette is all I can see and then he stalks off to the right. He's heading for the washrooms...

Declan

The woman is driving me crazy. I should have left her in the middle of the road where I found her. Not only will she bring war to the clan, one that I will relish, but she's also bringing an internal war that I have to battle on my own. That is the one that is bothering me. I would have loved nothing more than to take her into the shadows and have my way with her sweet cunt, but it's a little hard when one suffers from erectile dysfunction.

One minute my pecker is hard as a rock, and I feel like I could drive a hole through a brick wall with it, and the next second it's flaccid as a wet sock. Strangely enough since meeting her, what is it, two hours now? My dick has been hard more times with her in my presence than in the past year.

"Fuck!" I head across the empty room to the hallway, unbuckling my belt as I go. I can't get into the washroom fast enough and push open the first door on the right as I unzip my jeans. I slam into the room and lean back against the door as I pull my dick out and look at it like it's a monster with three heads or some shit. The tip oozes with pre-cum, and I'm in awe of it for some fucking reason. Probably because I haven't had a woody in close to a year.

Tentatively I start to stroke it from base to tip, waiting for the second when it deflates like a balloon with a fast leak. But it doesn't. It only grows harder, painfully so, as my balls start to tighten, needing to be released. I smack the light switch off and stagger my way over the sink. Leaning heavily upon it with one hand, I rub the precum down my shaft with the other and close my eyes.

Images of my little goose flash behind my eyes, and I can feel the tension building as I pump my hips back and forth. I wish now that I had taken her to that dimly lit corner so badly and had my way with her that I could hear her calling my name.

"Declan?"

My eyes spring open, and I look towards the door...

Wren

I went back to the table and was sitting there

munching on the food that Ginny had brought to the table. I asked her if those were boots that were in the gift shop, and she assured me they were. Handcrafted by a local with a price tag of a thousand bucks. Too steep for my blood. That was fifteen minutes ago, and I have to wonder if Declan is alright.

I snag a mozzarella stick from the platter and get up to go in search of him. Munching on the gooey stick, I enter the darkened room and pad across the floor in my sock feet to the beacon of light in the hallway.

Stopping outside of the men's washroom, I lean my ear against the door and hear nothing. I glance down at the crack between door and floor and see there is no light on. Pushing it open, I take a step inside. The room is empty. Leaning back into the hallway, I look further down and hear the sounds coming from the kitchen, and I wonder if he went in there.

But a loud thump against the women's door has me spinning around, thinking he's standing behind me. But he's not there. No one is. I'm torn between opening it to see if the lady in the washroom needs help and finding Declan. That was until I heard a groan on the other side of the door followed by, "Little goose that feels soooo fucking good."

Staring blankly at the door, I stuff the rest of the mozzarella stick in my mouth and chew rapidly as I push the door open.

Declan is standing there leaning against the sink with his head back, his skin shining in the dim light from the hallway. At first, I thought he was sick.

But being sick wouldn't feel so fucking good as he eloquently put it.

I call out his name. Three times before it registers. In his defense, I was choking on the mozzarella stick for the first two, but the last one came out just fine. Because he turned those ravenous eyes on me again, and this time without a doubt, I knew that look was for me.

"Get in here!" he growled as he took a step towards me, and I, him. We meet in a flurry of sexual pent-up frustrations. His hand grabs my face as he guides it towards his mouth as his other works his cock.

There are no meek tentative kisses from him. The second his mouth finds mine, he plunges his tongue inside, seeking out mine. They tangle in a dizzying, breathless dance until I feel the need of oxygen and lean back.

I push him against the wall and whisper, "Let me," as I place my hand on his and take over stroking his silky member. To say I didn't want it between my thighs, pumping in and out of me was an understatement, but this wasn't for me. It was for him. A few strokes in, and I can feel his body start to tighten all over. I drop to my knees and pray no one comes in as I take him into my mouth.

He takes a handful of my hair in each of his hands as he rams into my mouth, and I know he's starting to go over the edge as he freezes mid stroke. A guttural growl escapes past his lips as he slowly pumps down my throat, and I swallow every drop.

Spent, he bends over and helps me off the floor then pulls me against his chest. "Thank you for that," he mumbles into my hair.

"Don't mention it. Ever." I pull out of his embrace and cross over to the wall, feeling for the light switch. My eyes search him out, and I glance at him. He's stuffing his dick back into his jeans, and I'm horrified at how broken he looks from my words. I feel the need to explain.

"When I say 'ever' it's because I've never done that before. To any man. I'm embarrassed at how much I enjoyed it." And with those departing words, I pull open the door and hightail it back to the booth. Covering my head with his coat, I lay down and will myself to go to sleep.

Declan

Giving her time to process what just happened, I left the bathroom feeling like a million bucks and went in search of Ginny. I found her in the kitchen at the end of the hallway and tapped on the swinging door.

She smiled and waved at me. "Come on in. How can I help you?"

"Do you carry any boots in the gift shop by chance?" I ask, watching as she puts a basket of French fries into a deep fryer.

She turns and wipes her hands on the towel at her waist and nods "We do. Your girlfriend was asking about them too. Did she tell you the price tag?"

I shake my head. "She didn't even tell me you had any. How much?"

"Well, it's a local chap that handcrafts them. He sells the pair for a thousand dollars." She chuckles, "To say that he doesn't sell many is an understatement."

"Would you happen to have, say, a size eight?" I'm guessing at her shoe size of course. From pushing her into the back seat, I got a good look at her feet. They weren't small but by no means were they large either.

"Let me get these fries cooked up and served, then we'll go take a peek!"

"No problem, I'll just wander that way." I nod.

As I make my way towards the gift shop, I can't believe the shift in my whole body. A year of pent up sexual frustration released in a matter of seconds. And Wren did that for me.

Believe me I have tried. Sitting in the family's strip clubs night after night. Even going as far as paying for lap dances from some of the sexiest women I ever laid eyes on never got my pecker even slightly hard. I owed my little goose, big time. I would buy her those boots and anything else her little heart desires. I just won't tell her why.

Chapter 8

Wren

I wake up shivering and can't figure out why it's pitch black. Then the familiar scent of cologne fills my senses, and I realize that Declan's coat is covering my face. I groan in agony when I pull it from my face and smell bacon frying. Every muscle is crying in protest. And then the events of yesterday slam into me like a heat wave, ending with me popping my cherry at knob gobbling. I swallow and my throat aches from the movement. Damn romance books never mentioned what it feels like after the fact.

I lay there for a full five minutes, staring at the underside of the table, counting all the shriveled-up gum left behind by past patrons. I prefer it at the moment rather than facing Declan. Speaking of which, I look across and see that he isn't laying down but in fact is sitting there, and my eyes zero in on his crotch.

I pop up like a jack in the box and a pair of fawn colored winter boots, with fur trim and intricate beading sit before me. I instantly fell in love with them.

"Morning." I hear him say, and I move the boots aside.

"Why are these here?" I ask, pointing at them.

"They're for you," he says, looking out the window at a truck pushing snow in the parking lot.

"I can't—"

He turns and looks at me. "You can, and you will."

I've never had anything so beautiful in my life. But was he giving them to me just because I needed something on my feet or for payment of services rendered?

"Declan I can't afford these. Take them back, please."

"You don't have to. Put them on. The roads are open so whenever you're ready we will be off. "

I'm not surprised he ignored me. He is the type of man that doles out orders and everyone jumps, but I wasn't giving him the satisfaction of seeing me jump.

I fold my arms across my chest and look out the window. The storm had passed, and the sun was just peaking over the horizon.

A rumbling hiss escapes past his lips, and he pushes off the table to stand. I turn and look at him with a raised brow and find him glowering down at me.

"Look, if we break down, as much as I want you in my arms, I'm not carrying you. Now I'm going to grab us some coffee for the road. You can either stay here and look at those boots all day, or you can put them on and come with me. The choice is yours."

He turns on his heel and walks away towards the counter without a backward glance.

I sit there and think about his intentions. It's not like he asked me to give him a blow job, I just did it. I glance behind me to see him standing at the counter, talking to Ginny as she sits a tray down along with a paper bag. He's reaching for his wallet with a tight smile on his face shaking his head. They're talking about me. I can tell because Ginny is glancing my way with a look of concern. She's probably wondering if they fit. And I have a strong desire to wipe that look off his face.

To hell with it. I grab the boots and tug on one then the other. Standing, I'm pleasantly surprised they are a perfect fit and reach for Declan's coat, stuffing my arms into the sleeves. Pulling my hair out from under it, I take a quick glance of our lodgings for the night to see if anything was left behind then head towards the counter.

A smile breaks the look of concern on Ginny's face as she sees me and asks, "Did he get the size right?"

I look at Declan and see his face is relaxed when he sees the boots on my feet. I smile at him, a silent thank you and say to Ginny, "He certainly did. They are beautiful."

"Glad to hear," she grins. "I'll tell the crafter he had a very happy customer. Well, he will know that once I give him the two grand." She chuckled. "Are you sure you don't want another pair?"

I whipped my head at Declan so fast I got a sharp pain in my neck. "Two grand?!"

He grabbed the tray and took the bag off the counter, raising it in a wave, he looked at Ginny. "Thanks for the hospitality and the muffins. Someday we might be out this way and stop in again."

He shoved the paper bag at me and took me by the hand, leading me to the door. "Say goodbye to Ginny," he muttered.

"Bye Ginny, thanks for everything." I waved, just as the door closed behind us.

Out on the sidewalk I shook my hand free and stopped. "You paid two thousand dollars for these boots?!"

He snagged me by the arm and tugged me along. "Yeah, one for each foot."

"There is salt everywhere, I can't walk in the snow with these! That's like a month's worth of rent!"

He stopped, his breath puffing white in the cold air. "Are you kidding me?"

"No, that's how much my rent is."

He runs a hand through his hair, and I swear for a second it looked like he was going to pull it out at the roots. Damn shame if he did, he has such gorgeous hair.

"I don't care about your rent! I meant… you know what, never mind. Take this." He held the tray, and I took it wondering just what he was up to. Spinning around, he bent down.

"What the hell are you doing?" I ask, looking at him.

"Get on," he barked.

"On you?!"

"Woman, you're trying my patience. Either you get on my back, and I give you a ride over to the car or I'm throwing you over my shoulder. Which will it be?"

Do you know how hard it is to climb on someone's back without the use of your hands? It's not an easy task.

Lifting my left leg, I laid it against his side then leaned my right forearm on his shoulder, putting a lot of my weight onto it. As he hooked his hand under the back of my knee. I lifted my right leg and wrapped my arm, the one with the tray in my hand around his neck just as he hooked his hand under the back of that knee. I felt like a crab perched precariously on a rock. How we didn't fall back with coffee raining down on us is beyond me.

"Get your arm out of my shoulder, would you?" he rasped.

"Sorry!" I quickly moved it, more securely around his neck.

He jostled me upwards so hard I thought I was going to fly over his head. That would be a real treat for the patrons still inside the restaurant to see.

I glance towards it and see a few people with their faces pressed to the windows laughing as Declan sets off towards the Caddy, and I smile at them.

Halfway I start to slip. I can feel it, and so does he.

"Hold on," he says, jostling me up again. Only this time when he does, his hands slip to hold my ass and a little thrill spikes down my spine.

"You know, you could have just driven the car over to the doors." I mumble against his head as he goes to the passenger side of the vehicle.

He chuckles, setting me down on the ground. "And miss copping a feel? I think not."

We've been on the road for a half hour now, sipping on our coffees, the muffins that were in the bag, consumed within minutes of striking out. And now I'm sitting here, watching the landscape pass by, wondering what my fate will look like now. He interrupts my musings when he asks, "How did you get messed up with those men back there?"

I turn to look at him and notice in the light of day his profile, and I'm momentarily flustered from gazing at it. The five o'clock shadow he's currently sporting draws my eyes to his jawline. A strong jawline it is, looking like it was carved out of rock. My eyes travel further to his lips. Perfectly centered between his chin and nose, and I have a strong urge to bite the bottom one. He turns his bourbon-colored eyes on me and raises his brows. He caught me staring, and I started to squirm in my seat.

"Well?" he asks.

Obviously, he mistook the look of lust in my eyes for something else, and I let out a sigh of relief.

"I was to get married to pay off a gambling debt owed by my father; God rest his soul. To whom, I have no idea. He never told me. Just that if I didn't, they would kill him."

"Your father is dead?" He starts to scowl, and I want to smooth the line away on his forehead.

"No. But after he told me I had no choice and they would go after my job, I told him he was dead to me."

He looks at me and nods. "Understandable. I may be a prick, but even I wouldn't use my daughter to pay off a gambling debt. Speaking of pricks"— he flicked the blinker light on and pulled into the right turning lane — "in a very short time you're going to meet mine."

Whipping my head around, I gawked at him. "Didn't I already do that last night?"

He glances at me, and a peel of laughter bursts past those luscious lips of his. "I thought we were never to mention that again. Ever. Is what I believe you said."

Like a fish out of water, I sit there opening and closing my mouth with nothing coming out.

The merriment he'd felt moments ago was now gone as he turned down a tree lined dirt road. In its place was a dark, angry look that settled on his face as he said, "The prick is my father."

Chapter 9

Declan

No matter how many times I leave and return to my childhood home, the estate that's been in my family for over seven generations, I feel sick to my stomach. Just turning down the tree lined road brings back memories of times that I would rather forget.

Despite my father being old and feeble now, he wasn't always like that. At one point, it was so bad living under his roof, that my mother packed our bags and moved us to her family home in Windsor. He was fine with it as long as we visited on holidays. It gave him a chance to live with his whore freely. My mother was told if she ever thought of divorce, he would come after me. Not to go live with him, but to kill me. That was until I turned eighteen, and he demanded that I return to the Toronto area to learn the family business. I still blame him for my mother's death.

"Where are we going?" I hear Wren asking. The unease in her voice pulls me from my thoughts.

I can't say I blame her. What, with me looking like I could rip the head off the closest person to me, while driving into a forest, I suppose could be perceived as threatening.

I force my face to relax, but not my body. That's one thing I can't do, and I look over to her. Fear stares me in the face.

I stop the Caddy in the middle of the lane. "This is my home little goose. If you don't want to stay here, tell me now, and I'll take you wherever it is you want to go. But if you stay, know that you will be under my protection." She would be under my protection whichever she decided, but she didn't need to know that.

She looks at our surroundings then back at me. "We are in the middle of a road, Declan… in a forest."

A chuckle passes over my lips as I shake my head. "It isn't a road, it's the laneway to the house." I point out the windshield to a pole a hundred feet ahead. "See that camera on the top? There's one on every pole. The second I turned down here, the household knew we were coming."

She twisted in her seat and looked out the back window. Turning back around, she softly said, "Oh."

"What will it be? Go someplace else or stay here?" I ask, willing her to say she will stay.

"If I go back to my apartment, they will just find me, won't they?"

I nod. Knowing that whoever is behind this already knows where she lives. "They will."

She heaved out a long sigh. "I guess I really don't

have a choice"— her hand quickly darted out, and she grabbed my thigh — "I didn't mean the way that sounded. I just don't want to be an inconvenience."

Not hearing a word that came out of her mouth, I stared at her hand. A few inches higher and she would have grabbed my dick. And now the fucker was liking the attention. Picking it up, I placed it on her thigh and patted it for some damn reason. "It's fine."

Needing to get away from her before I took her on the front seat in view of the camera, I stepped on the gas and took off. Rounding the corner ahead, I hung right towards the mansion and stopped at the gatehouse.

A short man came out, stuffing his head into a winter hat and smiled. "Mr. MacGallan! Nice to see you home."

I nod. "Radley. It's nice to be home. How has everything been?"

"Good, nothing amiss. Well, except when your father went missing. But all was good, he was hiding in a closet in the east wing."

"Right. I heard." I reached for the control on the visor and pushed the button, the gates before us opened, and I said, "You have a good day now."

As I drove through the gate, I could tell Wren was looking at me. Itching to ask me the business about my father, is what I'm betting. Since that was the second time, she'd heard one of my men mention that he was hiding in a closet.

I looked at her and noticed her hands clenched in her lap. "Spit it out."

"Why was your dad hiding in the closet? Is he afraid of something? Did the men after me find out where you live?"

I shake my head. "No. The house is huge, and he just gets lost sometimes."

Satisfied with that, she relaxed her hands and gazed out the windshield, her breath hitching in her throat. "Oh my...this is your home?"

I know what she's seeing as the forest ends. She's seeing the laneway sloping gently downward to the circular driveway in front of the black stone house with its tall white columns, like guardians on either side of the front door. And it all stands out like a sore thumb against the pristine snow. An equally black barn, housing some of the country's finest racehorses sits beside a fully stocked pond with weeping willow trees surrounding it. Now barren of all their leaves, the reed-like branches are encased in snow from last night's storm. In the winter when I was a kid, I always thought they looked like sentinel monsters protecting the estate. It all looks so formidable, just like the bastard that built it.

"Your house looks like a mausoleum." She made a sound in her throat, like she instantly regretted speaking her thoughts aloud and muttered, "Sorry."

"Don't be. I always thought the same thing."

I step on the gas and drive down the hill to the

side of the house, instead of pulling out front and letting one of the men park it in the garage. Normally I wouldn't care, but no one has cleared the snow away from the front of it. After the fiasco back at the restaurant with her not wanting to walk in the snow, I figure it's best to avoid that again. Not that I don't like her breasts pressed against my back. I loved it. But now is not the time to be getting a woody if I can help it. And the way it responds to her, I can't help it.

I turn the Caddy off and look at her.

"Before you go in there, you need to know some ground rules."

She looks back at me with wide eyes and nods her head. "Okay."

"Under no circumstances are you to leave this property unless you're accompanied by me. Don't engage with my father, just ignore him. And the only man that you're permitted to talk to is Connor. Got it?"

I knew I pushed it too far when she squinted at me and folded her arms across her chest. The last one was a bit much I agree, but I'm not the type of man to share. I want her for myself. She just doesn't know it yet.

She sat there giving me the side eye look for so long I thought she was at a loss for words for the first time since meeting her. Finally, she cleared her throat and said, "Why? Why can't I talk to anyone other than Connor?"

I reached for the door handle and opened it.

"Because I said so." I sounded like a fucking parent talking to their kid. But she was far from a kid, she had to be at least... "How old are you?"

"What?!" Her brows rose so high, that they disappeared under her bangs.

There was no way that I would be with a teenager. I wasn't completely immoral and having a relationship with someone that was in diapers when I was in high school was not one I wanted to be in.

I slammed my door shut and went around to the passenger side, opened her door and held out my hand. "I said, how old are you?"

"Why does it matter?" she asked, placing her hand in mine.

The second her feet touch the cement floor of the garage I drop her hand and groan. I shake my head as I lead the way to the door into the house, because for the life of me I don't understand what is drawing me to her. To even think of getting involved romantically with someone so... so. "Because it just fucking does."

I open the door and hold it for her to pass by me into the mud room. Grabbing a pair of new slippers off the shelf, I pull the tags off and shove them at her. "Put these on."

Without even questioning my order, she takes her boots off and carefully lines them up on the boot tray then slips the slippers on her feet. "I'll tell you on one condition."

I roll my eyes, as I take off my boots and set

them beside hers. "Of course, you will. What's your condition?"

"Why do you call me little goose?"

I chuckle as I slip my feet into my own slippers.

"Because Wren doesn't suit you. You remind me of a goose that comes to the pond out back every year. She has a saucy attitude… like you."

She smiled for the first time since I turned onto the estate's private road, brightening up the room and my day. And it was that moment that I thought to hell with how old she was. If I wasn't smitten before, I am now.

"I'm 31. An old spinster."

Relief flooded through me. I didn't show it, only nodded. "C'mon, I'll give you a tour of the place."

Chapter 10

Wren

As soon as he opened the door of the mud room to a short hallway, a heavenly smell assaulted my senses. I say that because my mouth started watering,

and my belly started rumbling the closer we got to it. At the end of the hall was the kitchen. Something that you would see in a magazine and wish was your kitchen.

A man was standing at one of the two islands in the middle of the floor, stirring something in a pot. Him and Declan were talking, but I wasn't listening. I was in awe of the countertops. Both were a shiny black marble with gold veining running throughout. And it wouldn't surprise me one bit if it was real gold.

One housed a farmhouse sink, the other a gas cooktop with an indoor grill. It was a handy setup, allowing the cook to fill a pot, and simply turn to put it on the burner. Both islands had stools at the far end of each, and Declan sat in one and motioned for me to join him.

"Connor, this is Wren. She's the one I asked you to

get the room ready for," he said as he held the back of the stool while I jumped into it.

"Hi Connor, nice to meet you," I smiled. "What are you cooking there? It smells divine."

"Nice to meet you too, Wren!" he smiled, setting a steaming mug of black liquid, topped with whipping cream and chocolate shavings in front of each of us. "This here is Seafood Chowder, you're not allergic to cod, salmon or shrimp, are you?"

I shake my head. "Not at all."

"Good because it's for dinner along with Blaa."

I looked at him wondering just what he meant by the word. When he wasn't forthcoming, I looked at Declan. "What is Blaa?"— and I point to the mug— "and what is this?"

He chuckled and took his mug by the handle. "Blaa is rolls and this," — he takes a sip — "Is Irish coffee."

"I've never had one, always wanted to try it though." As I pick up my mug and take a sip, I can feel Declan's eyes on me. The hot brew instantly warms me up. "Oh, that's tasty," I say, setting the mug down.

"You got a bit of whip cream on your lip there," Declan murmured in that velvety tone.

Instantly my tongue darts to the corner of my mouth. "Did I get it?" I ask, looking at him. When he doesn't say anything, I look at Connor who is looking at him giving him a weird look as he sets a napkin in front of me.

"Well? Is it gone or not?" I ask. Not waiting for a

reply, I snatch up the napkin and wipe my mouth and he turns to look at Connor.

Then it dawns on me why he was staring, and I can feel my face turn red. He was remembering last night while my tongue swirled around the tip of his dick. Sneaking a glance at his crotch confirms my suspicions. If Connor wasn't in the room, I think I might have just squatted down in front of him and went for round two.

I start to wonder why I have the sudden fascination of having his dick in my mouth, when I hear him say to Connor, "Where's my father?"

He motions to the wall behind us, and out of curiosity I swivel in my seat to see a bay of monitors installed on the wall. How I missed that coming in the kitchen is a wonder.

"He's having a nap. He laid down the second he heard you were arriving."

Declan sighed and nodded. "Right. Is everything on plan for next week?"

My brows shot up. What was happening next week?

"Yes sir. The club is getting ready as we speak."

"Great. I can't wait." I noticed the dry response passing his lips and now I was really curious what was going on. "C'mon, goose. I'll show you around," he said, moving to stand.

"Did you just call her—"

"Yes! Yes, I did," Declan hissed. "Call us when dinner

is ready."

He headed to the far end of the kitchen that opened into a large breakfast nook that flowed into an inviting sitting room. Overstuffed leather furniture was placed for conversation in front of a roaring fireplace.

"You didn't have to snap at him," I said, when we were out of ear shot, my gaze darting to the sofa. I would love to sit on it curled up with a book.

"If I were snapping at him the whole house would know."

From that room, one could see straight to the entryway, and he took my arm, steering me towards it. A grand staircase wound upwards to the second floor. But the two solid mahogany doors, leading to the outside were a sight to behold. Each held a beveled window in the shape of crescent moons facing inward. On either side of the doors and above were windows to let the light in.

He caught me staring at it all and waited until I got my fill before tugging me to a hallway on the right.

"Bathroom is there on your left." He pointed as we walked past it. "This takes you out to the garage." Again, to the left he motioned to a doorway with a short hallway.

"I thought the kitchen was off the garage?" I said, already losing my sense of direction.

"The other garage." He made a right and started down a set of stairs. "This is the bottom level."

And what a bottom level it was. A wide screen tv that looked like it would have a hard time fitting in my apartment hung from one wall and opposite it, in a semicircle, sat three comfy looking double sized loungers. A bar sat at the far end of the room with a pool table in front of it. The whole perimeter of the room was bright from the doors leading out to an open patio that was tucked nicely under the rooms upstairs. Beyond it, the pond and barn could be seen from this vantage point.

"Follow me," he said, crooking his finger.

We headed towards the bar where a doorway stood open and went through it. A bookcase sat on one wall and a closed door stood in front of us.

"What's this?" I asked, wondering if it was some sort of dungeon that he was going to stuff me in. He slid a picture to the side on a shelf and revealed a keypad.

"The code is 719290, in case I'm not here and you need to get inside."

I laughed. He was so serious when he said it. What could I possibly need behind that door?

The door slid to the side, and another stood before us. Only it was made of steel. "Same code for this one," he murmured as his phone started going off.

I silently chanted the numbers in my head as he pulled it out of his pocket. He was still looking at it as the steel door slid the opposite way of the wooden one, and I stood there with my mouth hanging open.

"What is this?" I whispered as I stared at the walls adorned with every imaginable weapon one could think of. Mind you, they were all behind glass but all the same they were there. "Why are you showing me this Declan?"

Distracted by his phone, he murmured, "Because if you haven't figured it out by now, you're not exactly out of danger by being here. Sonofabitch!!" He just looked up from his phone. "You weren't supposed to see those," he hissed as he pressed a button high up on the wall. Wooden panels covered them from view. "In case you need anything, you just press it twice, it will open both sets of panels."

I gawked at him then started laughing as I glanced behind me. "Got any candle holders in here? Because that's about all I know how to use."

He chuckled. "No, but I'll make sure there are some placed throughout the house." He must have sensed how shook I was because he said, "Honestly, I wasn't planning on showing you the weapons." He tilted his head towards a door that stood closed in front of us. "I was showing you through there. Someone must have forgot to close the panels when they checked one out. C'mon."

Snagging my sleeve, he tugged me along as he opened the closed door. He flicked on the lights revealing a living area with a TV, a kitchen area, and rooms off of it.

"A panic room or should I say rooms? Is this your apartment or something?"

He shook his head. "No, I have a room upstairs. This is a fully functional apartment. Self sustaining from the rest of the house. If the need arises, you get your ass down here. The house could burn to the ground, and this would still be safe. There's also a way out if need be. Through a tunnel system that takes you to a trap door in the guard shacks floor."

"Couldn't you also get in that way?" I ask.

He shook his head. "No. The only ones that know that it's there are my father and me. Not even the guards know."

"Then why tell me?"

He sighed. "I wasn't going to. I was only planning on showing you this." He looked around, avoiding looking at me.

Panic surged in me. What did he know that I didn't? "What's going on Declan?"

"That message I got a few minutes ago… It was Rory. There's a contract out on me and…"

"And what?!"

He reached out and took a lock of my hair, slipping it through his fingers. "You little goose. There's a contract out on you too."

I could feel my eyes bug out of my head. "Me?! Someone wants to kill me? You, I get, but me?!" I was hysterical at that point. I would never hurt a fly. Who would do such a thing? And then it hit me. "Worm lips, it's him, isn't it?"

Declan squinted at me. "What?! Who the hell is

worm lips?"

I blink at him like he should know. "My intended. The guy I hit over the head."

"Oh no." He flicked the light switch off and guided me out the door. "He's in a coma. It's his father that had the contracts put out."

"His *father?* The loan shark?"

He nods. "Yeah, the Scottish loan shark, Oscar McLean. The one that wants to move into our territory."

He closes the door, and I walk through the weapons room without a second thought into the main area and head straight to the bar. I spin the cap off the first bottle my hand touches and start chugging it down.

"Ahh, Goose, you might want to take a breather there."

The taste hits me as the last word leaves his mouth. Why anyone would make such a bitter foul-tasting drink is beyond me and I start to gag. Racing to the sink I start to retch, praying that I'll throw up. But I don't.

"What the fuck is that stuff?" I gasp. When he doesn't answer, I look at him and feel my eyes start to twitch.

He's trying desperately not to laugh. "It's Malort, a liquor known for its horrible taste. We use it for the new recruits as a gag."

"Gag is an understatement." Grabbing a towel off the bar I try to wipe the offending taste off my tongue, then rinse my mouth with water.

He raises his brows at me, his lips curling up at the corners. "You good now?"

"Yeah, except my stomach is on fire and it tastes like I just licked the bottom of someone's shoe." I stick my tongue to the roof of my mouth and suck it down, then lick my lips. "And oddly enough black licorice."

"Really? Now that is odd." He moved to stand beside me and before I knew it, my chin was in one hand and my ass in the other and that velvety tone of his was murmuring, "Let me taste."

Chapter 11

Declan

I devour her mouth. My tongue zings along her teeth before tangling with hers. It does taste like licorice I decide as I grind my cock against her. Hard as a rock. As if it remembered how she took my dick last night. It wants to taste too. But getting head twice in less than twelve hours is even too much for me to expect. I like my women submissive but on their terms.

Over her shirt, my hand finds her breast and she mewed like a kitten under my touch when I flick her nipple. I back her towards a wall as I take the hem of her shirt and start tugging it over head. She stands there, eyes wide, in a pink lacy bra waiting for my next move as I lean my forearm against the wall. Inches from her, I'm stumped on what to do. Do I take her against the wall, or do I take her to my bed?

When I do nothing, she reaches for my belt and tugs me closer, and I wedge my knee between her thighs. Through the trackpants I can feel the heat from her pussy against my leg, and I claw at the strap of her bra, tugging it from her shoulder. Her nipple played peek-a-boo with me from behind the pink lace as I palmed the weight of her breast in my hand. Tired of the game, I reach behind her and unhook the clasp. My eyes feast on her breasts. I'm mesmerized as goosebumps come to the surface of her skin and her nipples stand at attention.

"Do you want this?" I hear myself ask.

A wicked smile erupts on her lips. Her hand snakes around my neck, guiding me to her nipple. "You best believe I do, stud."

I laugh then flick my tongue over the tight bud. "Are you sure?"

"Gee, I don't know. Tell me, are you sure?" she asks, then plunges her hand down my jeans and begins to stroke my dick.

An animalistic growl erupts past my lips. "Fuck yes."

I pull that nipple into my mouth like I'm sucking on a milkshake. With every tug of her hand, I suckle it deeper into my mouth. She starts to dry hump my leg and when we are both just about to go off, I hear, "Well, now, she's a bit of a heifer, ain't she?"

We spring apart. Wren ducks down grabbing her clothes from the floor, muttering to herself that she's a goose and not a cow, and I turn around at the offending sound and snarl.

"Sonofafucking bitch! Get your crazy ass out of here old man!"

My father spins around. Slippers flying, house coat flapping with his bare ass showing as he hurries back up the stairs. And I have to apologize for his outburst.

I turn around to see her slipping her arms into her shirt sleeves. I rub the back of my neck and open my mouth and say, "I'm sor—"

"Well, that was a jackass move if I ever did see one. What the hell did you yell at him like that for?!" Her eyes flash daggers at me and it turns me on more than I already was. But this isn't the time to give in to that carnal craving I have for her.

With her arms caught in her sleeves I stalk towards her like a lion after its prey. She knows I'm mad and starts to back up only to meet the wall. Trapping her there with my body, I tower over her. She looks up at me with that damn defiant gaze of hers, and I can't resist. I'm leaning down without any thought. My lips are mere inches from her chin, and I so want to rake them across her skin. My voice betrays me, coming out in a raspy murmur as I say, "Coming from the woman who told her father that he was dead to her..." I can't resist her and end up nipping her earlobe. As I dart my tongue out, to soothe the sting away, I bend my knees a bit, rubbing my cock against her pubic bone. A soft moan escapes past her lips as I say, "I don't think you have the right to question how I treat mine."

I back away from her like she's a venomous snake. Because right now, one strike from her and I would be a puddle at her feet. I fasten my jeans, then run a hand through my hair. Fuck, what is wrong with me? I need to get away from her before I rip her clothes off. I spin on my heel and head straight for the patio door.

"You're wearing slippers and have no coat, where the hell are you going?" she asks.

"Out. Get Connor to show you the rest of the house and stay the hell away from my father."

I slam out the door and head toward the barn. The one solace in my crazy world. My cowboy boots and work jacket are waiting for me inside, that is if I don't break my neck before I get there. Cresting the low hill was a challenge but one I accepted. Slipping and sliding up it, was the exact thing I needed to get her off my mind. And when I hear the whinny of my stallion, Jasper, from the pasture she's almost forgotten. Almost.

"Hey boy," I call out as he prances about. He sees that I'm heading inside and goes into the open doorway to the inside corral.

The smell of hay and wood shavings greet my senses as I open the door, and I kick the damn slippers off my feet. I slip the boots on, grab my coat off a peg on the wall and stuff my arms into the sleeves.

"What are you doing in here sir?"

I turn to see Ian, the stable hand standing there with a pitchfork and an empty wheelbarrow.

Taking the handle of the fork from him, I say, "Go up to the house and get something to eat."

He looks confused as Jasper makes his way into the hallway. "But I'm not done."

"You are for the night, now git. I'll finish up here." I don't wait for him to take his leave before I grab the wheelbarrow and make my way to the stall that stands open. Shoving the tines of the fork into the shavings I methodically work my way through the pungent smell of horse piss and shit as Jasper follows me in and starts to nuzzle my hair.

Wren

I follow Declan to the doors but stay inside and watch him stalk across the patio onto the snow-covered ground. I don't see it, but there must be a path there because he follows it to a low hill. I watch him take one step just to slide back down. Despite feeling like I'm going to throw up knowing I could be killed at any second, I find myself laughing hysterically at him. He eventually makes it up and over, and out of sight and this overwhelming feeling of dread hits me like a ton of bricks.

Wanting nothing more than to hole up in a room, I turn away from the window and head for the stairs in search of Connor.

Once on the main floor, I head to the kitchen, and I'm glad to see he's still there.

He looks up at me from the dough he's cutting and gives me a tight grin. "Sorry about the interruption. Tomas got away from me."

I wave a hand as I lean on the countertop he's working on. "It's fine. You can't be everywhere at once."

"Yeah, well, I'm just waiting for Declan to have my head," he said, as he picked up a piece of dough and started rolling it between his palms.

"He will do no such thing; I'll make sure of it," I murmured. He snaps his head up, gives me a strange look but doesn't say a thing as he places the doughy ball into a baking pan. I'm curious about that look he gave me, and want to ask why, but instead say, "Tomas, that's Declan's dad?"

He nods. "It is. Scott is with him now."

Swallowing the bile pooling in my mouth, I ask, "Oh, who is Scott?"

He added another perfectly round blob to the pan. "He's one of the reapers."

I blink, not sure I heard him right. "A what?"

His head snapped up. "Ah, he's just a worker."

A wave of nausea hits me again, and I push away from the counter. "Is there somewhere that I can lay down?"

"Give me a minute and I'll take you to your room," he said, as he placed the last ball in the pan. He covered the pan with a clean dish towel and set it beside the cooktop. "These need to rise for a bit anyway."

I waited until he cleaned up the counter, then followed him to the opposite end of the kitchen to an archway that opened into the front foyer by the staircase.

"Is there anything I should know about Tomas?" I asked as we walked up the stairs.

"Ah, well, he's forgetful and old. There's not much to know about."

I chuckled under my breath. Well, that summed it up.

"I should check on him just to make sure Scott is still there." Once upstairs, he took a left and I followed. Looking down at the foyer and admiring the front door from this vantage point, I just about smacked into his back when he suddenly stopped. He looked over his shoulder at me and said, "I should probably show you to your room first?"

"Sure, that would be great."

He turned around and headed down the opposite end of the hallway. Passing a door, he said, "Declan didn't bring any luggage in, is your bag still in the car?"

"Um, no. I didn't have any luggage."

He stopped in front of the second door and looked at me like he wanted to say something than thought better of it. Turning the door handle, he pushed it open and flicked on a switch. The room flooded with lights from the bedside tables, and I was in awe. A king-sized bed sat in the middle of the room, not up against a wall, but like in the middle of the room. A wood fireplace sat along one wall and Connor walked right over to it and tossed a log inside. "I'll get this going for you, so it won't be too chilly when you go to bed."

"Oh, you don't have to do that," I said, glancing around. It was like I stepped into the bedroom of my dreams. A canopy of navy-colored sheers hung from the four postered bed, trailing to the floor. Which kinda creeped me out. My luck the old place had mice and one would crawl up it and decide to get cozy in the middle of the night. But I decided I'd give it a go, considering I always wanted to sleep in a bed like that since I was a little girl.

"There's a bathroom through that door," he pointed. And my snoopy nose followed.

I walked into an oasis. A huge clawfoot tub sat along one wall in front of a pane of glass overlooking the barn and pond. Two things popped in my head. One, how did they ever get it up the stairs and two, was I brazen enough to have a bath in front of a glass window? I would find out later tonight I decided as I looked at the double vanity. A mirror hung on the wall above each sink, and glass shelves held a toothbrush, razor and shaving cream. How thoughtful I thought as I gazed at the walk-in shower that had a waterfall head and massage jets. Perfect for getting those spots that I nearly had to stand on my head to clean in my shower at home. And if that wasn't enough, a handheld sprayer. I could live in this bathroom and be perfectly happy, along with the happy ferns that hung in macrame holders.

But one thing was missing and that was the throne.

Spying two closed doors in the wall, I went to the first one and opened it. It was a room, with one window, a toilet and bidet. Call me crazy, but I got a little bubble of excitement at the sight of it and couldn't wait to give it a go. When Connor left that was. I stepped back into the main room and wondered what the second door was for. A towel closet perhaps? Turning the handle, darkness greeted me. Feeling for a light switch, I flicked it on. A very masculine bedroom stood before me. Another king-sized bed on a raised platform stood against the wall. The comforter was a charcoal gray, pulled down, revealing black satin sheets. But it was the headboard that drew my attention. Mirrored and framed with soft lighting and oddly enough a bar, in the middle, that ran the width of it. This was not a guest room. It was Declan's. And for some strange reason I could picture us in the middle of his bed with me pressed up against that mirror, hanging on for dear life to that bar while he…

"Oh, you found Declan's room?" Connor said, coming in to stand beside me.

"Yup!" I squeaked out. I could feel the heat rising on my cheeks as I pressed my lips together.

He cocked his head to the side and looked at me. "Are you hot? Your cheeks are a bit warm looking."

"A tad. I think I'll lay down now."

I wait until he closes the door softly behind him to flop on the bed and grab the nearest pillow. Stuffing my face into it I start screaming the anxiety away. Lifting my face, I take a breather and roll onto my back as tears start to run down my face into my hair. Somehow, I drifted off to sleep, that was until someone started pounding on my door causing me to bolt upright on the bed.

Chapter 12

Declan

The sun is just setting when I climb the stone staircase and make my way into the sun porch tucked in the corner of the upper patio. Taking my boots off, I set them on the boot tray before making my way into the kitchen. I'm surprised to see it's empty. Connor is always buzzing around when it's dinner time. I glance towards the dining room and find it empty as well. Where the hell was everyone?

The soup pot on the stove is steaming away, and a pan of Blaa is sitting to rise and looks like it has been for some time. I head towards the living room to find it empty too. Walking towards the hall to the basement, I hear my father yelling from above. I sigh heavily. At my wits end with the man and his antics, I grab hold of the banister and take two steps at a time. Hanging a left, I stalk to his room where his door stands ajar. My hand stilled on its surface when I heard Wren laugh. Gently I pushed it open and saw Connor standing there with his fists at his waist, arms flapping like bird and Wren sitting on the floor with my father.

"A chicken?" she called out, laughing.

"No! He's a turkey!" My father looked at her and grinned. And it shocked the hell out of me. I hadn't seen that man smile since I was a kid.

Connor saw me standing there and dropped his arms to his side. "Sorry Declan. We… ah…"

Wren turned to look at me, her eyes sparkling with laughter, and I realized at that moment I would say nothing that would wipe that look off her face.

"It's fine Connor. I think the rolls are ready for the oven though."

"Oh crap! I completely forgot about them." He ducked out of the room and hurried off to tend to his buns.

"Here let me help you," Wren said, getting up off the floor. She bent down and put her arm around my dad's waist and helped him to his feet. "Now will you be joining us downstairs to eat?"

"Oh, I don't know. I'm kind of tired now," he said, wiping his brow.

Wren shot me an imploring look, like she wanted me to say something, anything to help with the situation.

Being a busy man, I never noticed how frail my father was until now. "It's fine dad, I'll carry you downstairs."

Relief settled on her face but was soon replaced with a questioning look when my dad said, "Where is

Nora, will she be joining us?"

I shook my head. "No dad, she won't be joining us, she died, remember?"

"You're a liar, she did not die. She took you and left to live in Windsor."

I sigh. We've had this conversation many times and every time it ends badly. "Yes, she did, ten years ago, maybe if you weren't such a—"

Wren grabbed my arm. "Let's go down to eat, shall we?" She walked over to my father and guided him to the door. As they passed by, she said, "After dinner we need to talk. Now come on and help me get your dad downstairs."

"Oh, I'm stuffed," Wren said, patting her stomach. "That was delicious Connor. Thank you!"

I sit at the head of the table and watch with lazy eyes as Connor fucking blushes at the compliment.

"There's dessert too, don't forget!" he says with a grin.

"Oh, I couldn't," she sighs. "Well maybe, what is it?"

Connor stands and starts clearing the table, and says, "Chocolate cake."

She shakes her head. "Oh, it's tempting, but I better not."

With a keen eye, I take a sip of my wine when my

father pipes up. "Come on lass, you could use some meat on your bones."

Choking on my wine would have been better than it spewing out of my nose. Which is exactly what it did.

Wren jumps up, napkin in hand and says, "Good God Declan, are you okay?"

I snatch it out of her hand and wipe my face, before blowing my nose. "Son of a bitch, that burns!"

"What happened? Did it go down the wrong way?" she asks, taking her seat.

I give her a curt nod. "Yeah. You could say that." I push away from the table and look at the plate of cake that Connor set before her. "Eat your dessert. Meet me in the library when you're done."

I turned on my heel and left the dining room, trying to figure out how she had wrapped both men around her little finger in the time it took me to clean the stalls.

I'm sitting in one of the plush leather chairs before a roaring fire, sipping on a glass of cognac, my eyes glued to the door, waiting for Wren to join me. I glance at the mantle where the clock chimes ten times and wonder what the hell is taking her so long. I've been waiting for fifteen minutes. How long does it take her to eat a piece of cake?

Just as I think it, the pocket door slides open, and she walks in.

"Sorry it took me so long," she said, sliding the doors closed. "I had no clue where the library was."

My brows snap together. "Connor was supposed to show you around."

She flopped on the chair opposite me and nodded. "And so were you, but we know how that worked out."

I exhale loudly. "You told Connor I said to give you the tour, didn't you?"

"No. I told Connor that I needed to lie down because I felt like I was going to throw up."

I squint at her. Trying to read her face. I have to admit, she's got quite the poker face. Almost unreadable… almost. I can tell something is bothering her. Was it me coming on too strongly? Hell, that couldn't be it, she's the one that fell to her knees in the bathroom at the restaurant. So, what was it? "Did my father say something to you?"

"Not at all. Your father is a sweet man."

A laugh of derision slips past my lips. "Yeah, okay."

It was her time to squint at me. "When was the last time your father saw a doctor?"

I shrug. "I don't know, a year or more."

Her brows rose. "A year or more? Declan, he needs to see one soon. How long has he been like this?"

"Like what? Forgetful? I don't know, about a year." It just dawned on me. My ED started shortly after, around the same time. For fuck's sake. Was my erectile dysfunction caused by the stress of dealing with him? Could it really be that simple? "What makes you think he needs to see a doctor?"

She crossed her arms over her chest. "Well, I'm no expert, but I suspect he has dementia. Unless of course he always runs around the house bare assed?"

Thinking she meant down in the basement I said, "He had his robe on."

"He wasn't when he came pounding on my door while I was laying down. I opened it thinking it was you. Instead, I'm greeted by a wrinkly old wiener. Literally." She hiked herself up in the seat and shuddered. Shaking her head, she said, "I don't ever want to see that again."

If she wasn't so serious, I probably would have laughed in her face, but she wasn't joking. "Did he do something inappropriate?"

"No. He was lost. I can't imagine someone who has all their faculties getting lost in a house they've lived in, for how long?"

"Okay, I get it. I'll get Connor to make him an appointment." Seeing her smile was all the encouragement that I needed. I get up and move over to the liquor cabinet and pour her a glass of cognac and add a drop of water. Taking it to her, I hold it out. "So, what else is bothering you?"

She takes the glass and then a sip. "Oh, that's smooth." The tip of her tongue darts out, and she licks her lips.

I can't stop looking at her and murmur, "It's the water."

She looks at her glass then up at me. "What?"

I shake myself from the trance she has on me and go and sit in my chair. "I put a drop of water in it. It makes the cognac smoother."

"Oh. I would never have guessed it. As a matter of fact, I thought for a second you were losing your marbles." She laughs and sets the glass on the table beside her.

"Spit it out little goose. What's bothering you?"

She stares at me for a full minute before she finally says, "Someone is going to try to kill me, and there's not a damn thing I can do about it. Because I don't know who or when it will happen."

I lean forward and cover her hand with mine. "I told you, you're safe here. No one is going to kill you, Wren. Not while I'm breathing."

She looks away then swings her gaze back to mine. "You might not be breathing for much longer either. Remember they're after you too."

I burst out laughing, clearly, she has no idea what I'm capable of. And that's fine, I'll keep it that way.

I lean back in the chair and look at her with lazy eyes. I'm so tempted to throw her on the floor in front of the fire and finish what we started downstairs earlier but instead I say, "I suggest you get some rest. You're going to have a busy day tomorrow."

She's tipping her empty glass up, catching every drop of the liquid on her tongue and looks at me. When she sees that I'm watching her she sets the glass down on the table and gulps. "Doing what?"

I hold my hand out for her to take and when she does, I pull her up to stand. "We're going shopping. You need clothes and a gown."

She clutches my hand like a vise. "A gown? I don't want a gown! The last one I wore got me into this mess. Why the hell do I need a gown?"

I chuckle. "Relax. This one won't be getting you into any more messes. My swearing in ceremony is in less than a week, and you're going to be there by my side."

"Swearing in ceremony? For what?" She starts to shake her head. "I'd rather stay here... I'll watch your dad."

Her response set me back for a second and then I realized she was afraid.

"My father will be there too; everyone will be there. The ceremony is for me to take over his place as Captain. And having you by my side is the only way I can keep you safe."

I give her a nudge towards the door. "Now go get some sleep. We leave at daybreak."

She leaves without a backwards glance or a word, which shocks the hell out of me, and I pour myself another drink.

I sit in my chair and stare at the flames in the fireplace. With each passing second, she's growing on me more and more. If she had insisted on staying home, I would have relented and a few of my men would be staying with her. Because word on the street according to Rory was that a plan of attack was under way.

Chapter 13

Wren

This is the second time in as many days that I stand before a mirror staring at myself wearing a dress. "I don't like it." I say, looking at Declan in the mirror.

He's sitting there on a couch sipping coffee, watching me try on dresses. Why? I have no idea because every single one that I've tried on, and there's been ten, he likes but I feel like a sack of potatoes in it. I think he just likes to watch me suffer.

"How about this one?" The manager of the store asks as she holds out a turquoise, sequined strapless gown.

I wrinkle my nose. "No thank you. I'd rather not look like a disco ball. I'll just take a look around." I step off the dais and head towards the sales floor. If I had my way, I would wear a pair of jeans and a sweatshirt, but I knew somehow that wouldn't fly with Declan. Not when he took me to the most expensive clothing store in downtown Toronto.

I gravitate to the dress pants and start sifting through them. It didn't help that most of the clothing in the store was made for thin women despite having plus sizes. Of course they would look fantastic on someone slim.

"May I make a suggestion?"

I jump and look at the person standing at my elbow. A young woman with plump rosy cheeks and silver hair with pink highlights is looking at me with a smile pasted on her ruby lips.

"Sure," I nod. "Anything to get me the hell out of here would be great."

She crooked a finger at me, and I followed her. "We just got a shipment in and I'm unpacking it now and noticed your predicament." She pushed a black curtain aside, and I trailed behind her down a short hallway into an open room. "Here we are."

She picked up a black garment and held it up. A jumpsuit unfolded before my eyes. "It's a bit wrinkly but if you like it, I'll steam those out for you." She handed it to me and pointed to a closed door. "The staff bathroom is right there, go try it on."

I was never the jumpsuit kinda gal, couldn't stand the flared legs but not to be rude, I went into the washroom and closed the door and silently cursed. The plan was to stall for time then come out saying it wasn't the perfect outfit but there was no full-length mirror. I had no choice but to try it on and then go look at myself.

Quickly I stripped off my borrowed Declan clothes and put my feet into the legs. Pulling it up, I was surprised to see that it was an off the shoulder, sweetheart neckline with a fuzzy edge. Settling it around my shoulders and making sure my boobs stayed in as best as I could, I opened the door and stepped out.

Janice claps her hands together. "Oh, I knew it would be perfect the second I saw it!"

"You're kidding me, right? My boobs are threatening to fall out, and it's a jumpsuit!" I practically spit the word out.

"No, I'm not. Look!" She takes me by the shoulders and steers me towards a back wall. "Do you mind?" She asks, putting a hand to the clip in my hair.

"Go ahead." I nod.

She pinches the clip together and my hair pools around my shoulders, and I stare at my reflection in awe. By damn it, the girl was right.

"Now with the right necklace, a little makeup and a proper bra, all eyes will be on you."

I looked at her like she was nuts. What the hell kind of person did she take me for? "I don't want *any* eyes on me!" Well, that wasn't true, the only eyes that I wanted on me were bourbon colored. And the owner of those eyes was currently yelling my name.

Janice jerked her head towards his bellowing voice. "If I had that man and your assets," —she gestured to her flat chest— "I would be flaunting them."

"Fine, against my better judgment I'll trust yours, but only if you can find me a bra that holds me."

"Deal!" She grinned as Declan came scowling into the back room.

"Geezus Declan, what the hell is wrong with you?" I asked, crossing my arms over my chest. Which wasn't such a good idea because that drew his attention to the swell of my breasts.

His eyes darken and zeroed in on my face. "She will take it," he grumbled, then spun on his heel and headed out through the doorway.

Janice grinned. "See, I told you."

Janice was quite the sales lady. Not only did she find the perfect bra, but she also found a pair of closed toed, black and red gradient pumps with a gold heel. I knew what I'd be doing for the next couple of days, walking around the house breaking them in so I don't make an ass of myself on his night.

With the shopping bags safely stowed in the back seat, we get in his Caddy. He holds out his cellphone to me. "Here take this."

I take it and look expectantly at him. "And do what with it?"

He starts the car and pulls away from the curb after we buckle up then glances at me. "Are you hungry?"

I nod. "I could eat."

He stops at a red light and points out the

windshield. "Taco Bell, alright with you?"

I look to where he is pointing. "Sure." I hold up his phone. "What do you want me to do with this?"

"I was going to take you shopping for more clothes, but something has come up."

It's then that I notice the scowl on his face. Now that I think about it, it's been there ever since he came looking for me in the back room of the clothing store. "What's going on Declan?"

The light turned green, and he slowly accelerated, but was watching the rear-view mirror. "Nothing. Just go on Amazon and buy whatever you need. I'm already logged in."

I turn around in my seat and look at the car behind us. A black Nissan Pathfinder is right on our bumper and panic surges in my chest. "Are we being followed?"

He nods. "Yeah, that's Rory."

I turn to face the front and a whoosh of air escapes my lungs. "Thank goodness! I just about pissed myself on your leather seat."

That got a chuckle out of him as he flicked on his signal light and pulled into the Taco Bell parking lot. "We will eat in the car on the way home," he said, heading towards the drive thru. "What do you want?"

"Whatever you're having," I murmured, looking out my window. I grab his arm as a kitten darts out of a bush in front of us. "Stop!"

I unbuckle my seatbelt and push open my door and

scurry around the front of the car.

I can hear the whirring of his window lowering and I snap my gaze to him.

"Shh! You're going to scare it!"

"Get the hell back in the car, goose."

The kitten is frozen for a second and I make my move to try to snatch it. Only it was quicker and climbed up the side of a garbage dumpster where it proceeded to eat out of a ripped open garbage bag.

"Wren, I said get the hell back in the car. Now!"

I jumped at the tone of his voice and like a scorned child, I went back to the car dragging my feet.

Settling in my seat I looked at him and said, "I'm sorry, when I see a stray cat, especially a kitten, I just have to try to save it. Will you at least help me catch it? Please?"

He laughed. "I can't stand cats; they are nothing but a menace."

I nod and drop my gaze to my hands. For the first time since meeting him, I found something that I hated about him.

After getting our food, we ate it on the way home while I searched for clothing online. Consulting him on every item I put into his Amazon cart I closed my eyes and placed the order just as we pulled onto the laneway of the estate. Never in my life have I spent over $3000.00 at one time on anything, and here I was blowing that in a touch of a button.

"I can't believe I just did that. Somehow, I'll pay you back Declan. For everything."

He looks at me and smiles as he steps on the gas. "Don't worry about it. Any of it."

"I insist." I murmur and look out my window to see that we are already out of the woods, then back at him. "Even if it means taking care of your dad. That is my job after all."

He squints and says, "Who told you that was your job?"

"No one. That's my actual job. I'm a support worker for the elderly, remember? That's how I knew something wasn't right with your dad."

He pulls to a stop in front of the mansion and looks at me. "Well, if it makes you feel better, he has a doctor's appointment next week."

"Good, he needs to be diagnosed properly so you know where you stand with treatment." I unbuckle my seatbelt and reach for the door handle. "Aren't you going to shut the car off?"

He unbuckles his seatbelt and pushes his door open. Coming around to my side, he opens my door and holds his hand out. Immediately, suspicion enters my mind.

"What are you doing?" I ask as I place my hand in his, and I swear my feet hadn't even touched the ground and he was shuttling me to the front door.

"Nothing." He shoves the front door open, and Connor is standing there with a worried look on his face.

"Connor, get the bags out of the back seat, would you?" Declan says as he continues to tug me along.

I shake my hand free of his. "What *the fuck* is going on?" I demand.

Chapter 14

Declan

After making sure Wren was inside and would stay there, I head back out to the car and hop in. I wasn't entirely sure she wouldn't run after I refused to get the damn cat for her. She looked so sad that I almost caved but couldn't. Nor did I tell her where I was going. She did not need to know that one of our warehouses had its roof blown off while she was trying on dresses.

Apparently, it was a warning from Oscar McLean. Letting me know that the war was on. Well, if it was war that he wanted, war is what he was getting, only I wasn't giving a warning.

"Call Rory," I say aloud, and the sound of the phone ringing goes over the speakers.

He answers on the second ring. "Hey Declan."

"Send me directions to the hospital," I say in way of greeting.

He knows exactly what I'm talking about, and when I hear the ping of it being sent, I'm just turning on the highway. Swiping the screen, I open the message and set it as my destination. "Now, tell me who told you it was McLean that blew the warehouse?"

"He did."

"Care to elaborate?" I scowl, for a couple of reasons. One, why would Rory be talking to McLean, and two, I always suspected there was a mole in 'the family' but never for a minute thought it would be him.

"I was down at the club on Yonge Street, checking things out like you asked, and he walked in. Spouting his mouth off that he personally was the one that set the charge and detonated it."

Relief washed over me as I sped towards the hospital. "Nothing like getting it from the horse's mouth," I said. "Meet me at the hospital. I'll be there in twenty minutes. I need a distraction."

"Sure thing boss," Rory said, and hung up.

I tap the screen and find Judgement Day again and let it blast as I get myself psyched up.

Twenty minutes later on the dot, I pull along the curb on the street behind the hospital and text Rory, letting him know where I am. Ten minutes later, he passes by me and finds an empty spot, two cars ahead of me. I watch as he gets out of his Pathfinder and puts money in the meter before he makes his way to me.

He pulls the door open and gets in, slamming it shut. "So, what's the plan?" he asks me.

"What room number is it?"

He pulls his phone out of his pocket and flips through his text messages and says, "411."

I nod as I look out the window. "When I get out of the car, set a timer on your phone. Give me twenty minutes." I look at him then reach across to the glove compartment and open it. Taking the gun from within, I feel for the silencer and grab it, twisting it on the end. Checking to make sure the safety is on, I say, "Whatever you can do for a distraction you do it."

Rory raises his brows at me. "What are you going to do about cameras?"

He's got a point. Unless I shaved my head afterward, it wouldn't be hard for me to be recognized and I was partial to my clean cut, chestnut waves. I looked in the backseat to see Connor had missed a bag, grabbing it, I stuck my hand in and pulled out a woman's wig.

"Where the hell did that come from?" Rory chuckled.

I look at him dumbfounded. "Fuck if I know. I took Wren shopping and don't remember her getting a wig."

I stuck it on my head and tugged it into place. Looking in the mirror to make sure my hair was covered, I turned to Rory. "How do I look?"

He burst out laughing. "Sexy, all you need is some lipstick."

"Fuck off." I snag the ball cap from his head and plunk it on top of the wig, tugging it down to hold it in place. Opening the center console, I pulled out a pair of sunglasses and put them on. I look at him over the rims. "Remember twenty minutes starting now."

I open the door and climb out. Lifting the back of my coat, I tuck the pistol into the waist of my jeans and head off towards the hospital.

The smell of antiseptic fills my senses as I enter through the sliding doors, and I keep my head down as I make my way along the hallway to the bay of elevator doors. Pressing the up button I wait, eyes forward until I hear one open to my left. Thankfully the other ten people that were waiting along with me, entered as well.

"What floor?" A man in his early fifties said aloud. People started calling out the floor they wanted, then he looked at me.

I looked back at him like I did Rory, over the rim of my glasses and said, "Third." No reason to tell him exactly which floor I was heading to.

Once the elevator came to a stop on the third floor, I exited and walked down the hall and noticed a camera roughly every thirty feet. Just passing one, I took ten steps and ducked into an open door on my right.

Luckily it was empty. Well not quite. It wasn't exactly occupied, but it did have clothes inside cubicles. It was a changing room for diagnostics. I wasn't a complete prick. I wouldn't steal another's clothing just to disguise myself. But I would steal a hospital gown. And there was a stack of them on a metal shelf at the end of the hallway. Next to it, was a cupboard with a bunch of papers on it and a pair of scissors laying on top of them.

Taking off my coat, I glanced at the doorway to see if anyone was coming in, then opened the middle door and stuffed the coat inside and tossed Rory's cap on top before closing the door. Quickly I put on a gown backwards, then another like a housecoat. Normally I wouldn't be so careful, but this was not a normal job for me. I'd never offed anyone in a hospital before, it's always been away from any prying eyes. Not that I'm worried, far from it. But this would be something the cops wouldn't turn a blind eye to.

I gather the lengths of the wig in one hand and the pair of scissors in the other. I'll have to buy Wren a new wig because I cut a good twelve inches off and tossed it into a hamper. Taking two more gowns off the shelf, I shake the folds out of them and toss them on top. Checking to see if the gun is still securely tucked into my jeans, I head out the door.

I find the stairs and take my time going up to the fourth floor. Any minute now, Rory's distraction should be going off. I should have been more specific on the distraction, but Rory was a creative guy. I'm sure he would come up with a good one. Just as I thought it, the floor rolls beneath my feet and I almost stumble into room 411. I'm wondering what the fuck Rory did when the fire alarm goes off.

Wasting no time, I enter the room and hear the machines before I see the man laying on the bed. I pull out a pair of gloves from beside the door and put them on, kinda hoping Oscar will be visiting his son, take both out at the same time, but no such luck. I walk further into the room and stop at the foot of the bed, taking the clipboard hanging from it. I glance at the name and see that it's Colin McLean, definitely his son and according to his chart, this is the best life he will live. I look at him and the life support machines keeping him alive. Wren really must have smashed him on the head, I'll need to keep that in mind if I ever piss her off. And now, I'll finish the job... for her.

Deciding against using my gun, I grab a pillow from a nearby chair and set it on top of his chest then yank out the intubation tube from his mouth. If I had a knife, I would cut off his middle finger and use it to leave a message. Instead, I pull the IV from his arm, and dip my gloved finger in the blood spurting from his vein. The tangy smell of metallic fills the room as I start to write on the pillow. Three letters... W A R.

I wipe my finger clean under the word, as if I'm underlining it then prop the pillow above his head. I check to see if he's breathing and when I'm satisfied, he's not, I head out the door and retrace my steps to the third floor.

∞∞∞

The sun was setting by the time I exited the hospital. The lights from the firetrucks and police cars lit the vicinity and I could see Rory leaning against the Caddy, his arms folded across his chest with a stupid grin on his face.

"What the hell did you do, man?" I ask, as I get within earshot. "Get in."

He rounds the hood of the car, and we pile in at the same time. "Here." I pull his cap from my coat and toss the wig in the back seat and hand it to him. "Now, tell me what you did that made the floor quake under my feet?"

"I didn't do anything. Well, that's not true, I pulled the fire alarm, after I put an oxygen tank in the janitor's closet."

I look at him. "And?"

"And, I may have knocked the valve off just a bit after I set it at the far end and left a lit match on the floor."

I shook my head. "You're lucky you didn't blow up with it."

He nodded. "Don't I know it. Oh, Connor called while you were in there. It seems Wren isn't feeling well."

"What's wrong with her?"

He shrugged his shoulders. "Don't know."

I start the engine thinking she's probably just worried again.

Chapter 15

Wren

Connor asked me what I wanted to eat for dinner after Declan left, and I told him to surprise me. Which he did, with a lovely steak dinner. Complete with a baked potato smothered in butter and sour cream, sautéed mushrooms, and asparagus along with a nice crusty loaf of garlic bread. And I couldn't eat a bite of it. The second he set it down in front of me, vomit pooled into my mouth. Which really pissed me off because I was starving. And now here I lay in my bed, sweating my ass off and freezing at the same time. Like how is that even possible? I'll tell you.

Running back and forth from the bed to the toilet because of the green apple splatters, that I just know was from the Taco Bell we had eaten for lunch, that's how. But the pain in my stomach can only be from my PCOS, something that I was born with but didn't come to light until I hit puberty. Thank God for small miracles. Not. I wouldn't wish this upon my worst enemy. Between having no periods to light ones to extremely heavy ones that sometimes last for weeks, it's pure hell. And it's been a while since I had a heavy period, and I think this one is going to be a doozy. So much in fact that I had to swallow my pride and shame to ask Connor to go buy me some pads.

The look on his face when I said extra thick ones, the thicker the better was hilarious, and I would have laughed in his face if it weren't for the pain. I thought he was going to faint when I asked him to throw in some waxing strips while he was at it. The poor guy probably thought I wanted to wax my coochie. Which, if I were intimate with a certain Irish man, I would likely do it, but no, I noticed the other day that annoying fuzz starting to grow back on my upper lip and chin. With Declan's swearing in ceremony in a few days, there was no way I was going with more hair on my face than him.

I whip the covers back as a hot flash feels like it's burning into my soul and pray to God that it will soon pass. Sweat pools between my breasts, and I feel the need to get in the shower, but I don't have the strength to move, not even my eyes when I hear a knock on the door.

"Meh," is all I can get out and the door cracks open.

"Here is the… Stuff you wanted," Connor says, as he enters. He comes over to the bed and looks down at me. "Are you okay? You're not looking too good."

"I feel fine," I mutter. Not wanting to tell him what the real problem is.

"I'm going to call Declan," he says, as he pulls out his cell phone.

"Don't you dare. This is… Oh God!" I dart out of the bed as my bowels start to do the tango in my gut and push past him to the bathroom door. "Get the fuck out of here," I roar in agony as I slam the door shut, yank my pj bottoms down and plop my ass on the toilet.

I hear the sound of his feet pounding across the wooden floor and the door slamming closed just as round three of the green apple splatters commences.

Declan

Connor is standing at the kitchen counter when I enter the kitchen from the mudroom, with a look of pure horror on his face.

"What is it?!"

He looks up at the sound of my voice. "I had to go buy her pads… thick ones. I don't think she's feeling very good."

I chuckle at the seriousness of his voice and walk over to the shelf and grab a glass. Turning on the tap, I let the water run cold before filling it up. "Why's that?"

"When I brought her the pads, she told me to get the fuck out."

I drink the water then nod. Sounds about right.

"Well, it was more like a carnal, agonizing scream. I think you should go check on her. Like now."

I sigh. After doing a hit I always need to unwind with a glass of brandy. Always replaying the scenario through my mind. But this time apparently, I can't, because Connor is giving me the evil eye.

I raise my hands in defense and notice blood on my hands. How it got there I have no idea, considering I wore gloves the whole time. "Fine." I turn the tap on, grab the container of dish soap, squirt some into the palm of my hand and start to scrub. "I'll go. But you better have a glass of brandy waiting for me in the library when I get done."

Drying my hands on a paper towel, I head towards the front foyer and climb the stairs two at a time. Walking down the hall, I pause outside Wren's door and press my ear against it. Not a peep was to be heard. I turn to retrace my steps and then I hear her groan.

I turn the doorknob and push it open. It's dark, save for a small table lamp closest to the bathroom door.

"Wren?" I whisper in case she's sleeping.

When all I get is more groaning, I move to the side of her bed and see her hair is wet and her face beaded with moisture. I lay a hand on her forehead and find she's burning up. "Sonofabitch," I mutter.

Leaning down, I rub a hand over her shoulder. "Wren, what's wrong?"

She shakes awake and stares at me with fevered eyes. Eyes that look straight through me.

"I'm so cold and the pain," she whispers, teeth chattering.

"That's it." I whip the covers back, lean down and slide my arms beneath her. Gathering her close I make my way towards the door and head to the stairs. "Connor!" I yell.

He rushes to the foot of the stairs and looks up.

"Grab a blanket and start the Caddy. I'm taking her to the hospital!" I tell him as I make my way down the stairs. Her head lolls back like she's a rag doll as I pass through the kitchen to the mudroom.

"Cars started," Connor says, as he stands there with a fuzzy blanket in his hand, holding the door open.

I enter the garage and see the Caddy's passenger door is open, and I place her on the seat. I recline the seat then buckle her in before taking the blanket and tucking it around her. She starts to groan again, clutching her belly. Brushing my lips over her forehead, I whisper, "It's okay little goose, I'll get you some help." I close the door and round the front of the vehicle and hop in, reversing it before I even buckle my own seat belt.

I tear out of there and speed into the night towards the hospital. A different one then I'd previously visited.

Wren

My eyes flutter open and for a second, I haven't a clue where I am, but I have the sensation of moving.

Fast. Turning my head, I see Declan sitting behind the wheel of his Caddy and for the life of me I can't remember where we are going. Nor do I care, I just want this pain to go away. A wave of nausea hits me, and I mutter, "Pull over." I'm going to throw up, I can feel the bile rising in my throat. "Declan either you pull over now or I'm barfing all over your car."

Immediately, he slowed the car down and pulled off to the side of the road in the nick of time.

Chapter 16

Wren

The car comes to a rocking stop, and I hear his door bang and then feel a cool breeze on my face. Opening my eyes, I see Declan standing there beside me just as he bends into the car and unbuckles my seatbelt. He takes me in his arms and rushes inside the sliding doors.

A wild look is on his face as he stomps down the corridor and approaches a woman who is mopping the floors. "Get a doctor now!" he snarls, holding me tighter.

The poor lady jumps and scampers off, dragging the mop behind her as he follows her.

"I don't think she can get a doctor," I say, my voice barely above a whisper.

"She better hope she does," he muttered as he looked from left to right as we passed room after room. Rounding a corner he says to the woman, "Where the *fuck* is the emergency department?"

"You came through the wrong doors." The woman

came to a stop outside a set of elevator doors, she pressed the call button and said, "You're in the basement. Take this to the first floor. Once you get there, walk straight down the hall. The emergency department is at the end of it."

He mutters his thanks as he steps in, and for the first time I look at him. Worry and panic is etched on his handsome face, and I wonder how he has been able to carry me for so long. "Declan, put me down, I can walk."

The doors whoosh open, and he starts walking down the hall. He shakes his head. "Not until a doctor pries you from my hands will I be putting you down."

"I know what it is. It's PCOS, it happens all the time."

"What?!"

"Polycystic ovarian syndrome. I have medication for it, at... *oh God*...!" A wave of crippling pain hits me so hard that it leaves me breathless. "Forget I said that this is not right. I think something is —"

Declan

I looked down at her in my arms to see why she didn't finish what she was saying only to see the whites of her eyes. I quicken my pace to a set of closed double doors. Hitting the handicap button with my knee, I step aside for them to open and see a nurse coming through.

"Get a *fucking* doctor now before I start burning shit!" I say through gritted teeth.

"I'm sorry sir, she needs to register,"— she points to a desk behind glass — "Right over there. Just take a number and they will call you."

I look at her with menace and know that mayhem is just under the surface. I swing my gaze around for a safe spot to put Wren. When I find none, I look back at the nurse with a raised brow. "Did I stutter?"

"Ah… No." She takes one look at Wren's pollard skin and has the decency to look taken aback. "Follow me." She takes the keycard that's on a lanyard around her neck and swipes it and pushes inside, holding the door open. "Wait here. I'll be right back."

I watch her walk down a hallway to the back of the emergency department where she talks to a man wearing scrubs and a white jacket. He looks at me and our eyes meet. In no time he's coming down the hall. "What's the meaning of this?" he asks. Looking at the nurse that brought us back here he says, "Call security Joanne."

I hike Wren higher in my arms, and one hand snakes out, catching the doctor by the front of his jacket. With deathly steel in my voice, I look him in the eyes. "You help her now, or I promise you won't be going home tonight."

He turns all shades of red and looks like he's about to bust a vein in his temple when another doctor comes from the back. "Declan? What's going on?"

Doctor number one looks at the new arrival and sputters, "You know this—"

"Careful there, you're talking about my cousin," he said, stepping in front of the first one, dismissively. To the nurse he said, "Move the woman with the bandage on her finger to a chair and get that bed ready."

Mike Murphy was never one to get involved with the family business, he had other aspirations in life. Like helping the people that we maimed. And in that moment, I couldn't be more thankful that he'd chosen to be a doctor.

"Mike," I nodded. For the first time since discovering her in bed, relief replaced a smidge of my anxiety.

Pulling out a small flashlight and opening her eyelid, said, "Oh well, can't see anything there with her eyes back. What's her name and her symptoms?" he asked.

"Wren and um, I don't really know other than she threw up on the way here. She was clutching her belly and said something about PCOS?"

"The room is ready," Joanne said, as she came up behind Mike.

"Right, thanks Joanne, go on your lunch break now." He looked at me and said, "Follow me."

Once we got to the back of the emergency department, Mike pushed the curtain aside and told me to lay her on the bed. "You can go take a seat in the waiting room."

I gave him a look that said otherwise.

"Or you can just stand out of my way," he grinned, pulling the curtain closed.

"I think I'll stay," I said. Moving out of the way, I stood there with my arms across my chest, watching as he looked Wren over.

During the examination she came to, and her eyes searched for me. "Declan? Where is he?"

"Right here." I stepped forward and took hold of her hand.

"Hey there Wren, I'm Doctor Murphy, I'm just going to have a listen" Mike said, as he took out a stethoscope from his pocket and put the tips in his ears. Placing it on her belly, he listened for a full minute straight then took it off. "No rumbling going on. When was your last bowel movement?"

"Earlier tonight. We had Taco Bell, and it didn't agree with me," she said.

"That will do it." He chuckled. "Declan says that you were throwing up. How many times?"

"Just once on the way here."

"Right." He nodded and placed his hand on her belly and felt the left side of her abdomen. "Does that hurt?"

She squeezed her eyes shut. "Yes, but not where you're pressing."

"Hurts on the right side, does it?"

She bit her lip and nodded.

"Okay, I'm going to order some blood work to rule out a UTI and if that comes back clear, a CT scan."

"Is that necessary?" I ask.

Mike nodded. "To properly diagnose what I think it is, yes."

"Stop beating around the bush Mike, what the hell do you think it is?"

"Appendicitis." He pulled the curtain back and said, "Mia, can you come here?"

A short blonde nurse came over and Mike said, "Get an IV in her and do a full blood work, marked urgent."

"Absolutely!" She said, smiling at Wren.

"Declan," Mike raised his brows at me "You need to go register her now. Just go back the way we came."

Wren squeezes my hand as tight as she can. I know the feeling; I don't want to let her go either, but I have to.

Leaning close to her ear, I brush her temple with my lips and whisper, "You're in good hands. I'll be back as soon as I can."

She nods as I stand and let go of her hand. With one last look over my shoulder at her, I head towards the registration desk and stand beside it.

"You can take a seat sir, and I'll call your number," the man says, sitting behind a computer screen.

I glance around the room and see one empty chair beside a man holding a child with an extremely running nose. "I'm not taking a number. The woman I brought in, is in the back. I'm here to cover her bill."

The man raises his brows. "Oh. Does she have a health card?"

"Probably, but not with her." I reach for my wallet. "How much will it be?"

"That depends on the services needed." He grabs a laminated piece of paper and passes it under the window to me. Pointing at the cost of everything, he says, "It would be best to get a hold of her health card."

I pull out the black credit card and slap it onto his laminated sheet and slide it back under the window. "Charge everything to this."

He smacks his hand down, stopping me from sliding it further. "I can't take that; you will need to go to the accounting department."

I shot him an annoyed look as I picked up my card. "And where might that be?"

He points toward the hallway that I carried Wren down. "That way. But go up the staircase beside the bay of elevators, hang a right and down the hall to the very end."

I take a step to do just that, but he continues.

"Then you need to take the elevators to the fifth floor... Never mind, here, I'll just draw you a map."

Forty-five minutes later, after leaving my credit card number on file with accounting and registering her, I'm being buzzed back into the emergency room department. Hurriedly, I walk to Wren's bed. The curtains are wide open, and a young woman is sitting on her bed. "Who are you and what the hell did you do with Wren?!"

"Declan!" Mike said and motioned for me to come over.

"Where is she?!"

"You no sooner left, and she started screaming. I took her myself over to the imaging department. Her appendix is on the verge of bursting, she's up in surgery right now."

I grind my teeth and feel a muscle twitch on my jawline. "Where is that?"

Mike looked at the clock on the wall and said, "Give me twenty minutes and I'll take you up."

I shook my head. "I can't wait twenty minutes. I need to go to her now."

Mike scribbled something on a piece of paper. "No, you don't. It's an hour-long surgery at best, you're waiting like any normal person would. Go sit in that chair." He pointed to one beside a bathroom.

If it had been any person other than Mike, I would likely have punched the guy out. But instead, for once, I did what I was told and went and sat down. Then I called Rory to come move my car before it was towed.

∞∞∞

Twenty minutes later, Mike and I are walking down a hall in the basement of all places, and I have a feeling that the OR is not down here. "Where are we going?" I ask him.

"Cafeteria. Want a coffee?"

Feeling the need to be at least on the same floor as her, I bite out, "Why the fuck would I want a coffee when Wren is upstairs somewhere under the knife?!"

"Relax." Mike stops in front of a door and pulls on the handle, opening it. "There's nothing you can do up there anyway. And besides, this is my lunch break. Let me grab a coffee first, will ya?"

"Fine. One coffee, then you either tell me where to go or I'll find it myself. And you're not going to like it if I have to do that."

We walk into the empty cafeteria save for a woman sitting at a table, munching on an apple as she reads a romance novel. He smacks me on the back and laughs. "Haven't changed, have you Declan?"

"Never." I say, grabbing a paper cup. Sticking it under a large carafe, I turn the spigot on and fill it with the steamy brew. Trying to get my mind off of her and what she's going through I say, "Are you coming to the swearing in?"

"When is it?" Mike asks, looking at a vending

machine full of grab and go foods.

I grab a few sugar packets and a stir stick in one hand and pick up my cup in the other. "Supposed to be in three days. But with Wren in the hospital now, I'll be postponing it. How long do you think she'll need to stay?"

Mike lifted a shoulder. "Depends, could be a day or a week."

Silently, I nod. "Would she be good in three weeks, do you think?"

He pushed the buttons of his selection and opened the little door and took out a sandwich. "Probably. Most people are back to normal in a couple of weeks. Which reminds me. You said she was saying she has PCOS?"

I frown, wondering how that could remind him I'd mentioned it. "Yeah. Why? Did you see something on the CT scan?"

I followed his lead as he walked over to a table and pulled a chair out. We both sat down, and he unwrapped his sandwich and took a bite. Chewing, he said, "No. It doesn't show up with a CT. Anyway, between you and me, there are natural supplements that she can take to alleviate her symptoms."

I raised a brow as I dumped the packets of sugar into my coffee. "Such as?"

"I don't know, I'm a Doctor of Medicine not a naturopath. Google it."

Chapter 17

Wren

I'm slowly waking up, from a cloud-like, floaty sensation. I know I am because I'm very aware of someone groaning in pain nearby. I don't know where I am or who is with me, but I do know that they are in pain.

The groaning sound resonates through my chest, and I realize it's me and start to giggle. Why am I groaning? I have no idea because I don't feel a speck of pain. That was until I heard an overly cheerful voice say, "There you are Wren! How are you feeling?"

I don't want to answer her. I want to stay in this floaty sensation, void of everything. But the smell of the hospital floods my senses and I know exactly where I am and why.

"Are you feeling any pain?" the voice persists.

My tongue feels like cotton in my mouth, and I lick my lips. "Water," I croak out.

"Oh no, you can't have that until you wake up a bit more. I'll get you a sponge instead."

"What the hell is a sponge going to do?" A velvety voice interjects at the sound of someone hurrying off.

I know instantly who it belongs to. "Declan?" I whisper.

He slips his hand in mine and murmurs, "I'm here little goose."

"Get me out of here."

"I can't do that," he replied, his voice thick with emotion as I felt him smooth my hair back. "I almost lost you. You need to stay here for a few days."

I couldn't figure out what he meant by almost losing me. I shake my head. "I'm not lost. You found me, remember?"

"Yeah… I do. Get some rest," he murmurs close to my ear, and I'm out like a light.

Declan

"Here we are." The recovery room nurse announces as she comes back, holding a plastic cup of water with a stick in it. "Oh, she fell back to sleep?" She sits the cup on a tray and looks at me as she pulls the stick out, — "Here is the sponge,"— then drops it back into the cup with a little splash. "If she wants a drink again, just run this along her lips."

I look at her like she's insane but only nod. "How long will she be here in recovery."

She walked over to the machine and checked the readings. "Everything looks good. I would prefer if she were a bit more awake, but they will keep an eye on her upstairs." She looked at her watch. "We can move her in about fifteen minutes. If you want to go grab a coffee, you have time."

"I'll wait."

I didn't end up waiting. Instead of fifteen minutes it was going to be a lot longer. Until she fully woke up. Deciding to go get the suggested coffee, I brushed my lips against Wren's forehead and left.

On the way to the cafeteria, I passed a gift shop that was open. Stopping, I backed up and walked inside.

"Evening," the woman at the counter smiled. "Let me know if you need any help finding something."

I nodded. "Evening. Will do." I walked around the little shop, picking things out that I thought Wren might need. Toothpaste and a brush, lip balm, a magazine, and a tube of hand lotion. I made my way over to a display of plants and fresh cut flowers. I had no idea if she liked either but grabbed a cactus looking plant and a bouquet of mixed flowers in a crystal vase. Walking to the counter I set everything down on it and snagged a chocolate bar for good measure. Reaching for my wallet, I looked around. "Do you have any gum?"

"Sure do," the woman pointed and laughed. "Right there in front of you."

I sighed. "Right."

"Long day?" she asked, as she rang up the stuff.

"Very." I yawned. "And it's not over yet."

She bagged up my purchases as I tapped my debit card on the machine. Taking the bag from her, I mumbled my thanks and headed to the cafeteria.

An hour later, Wren's awake, and they are getting her settled into the bed of a private room and she keeps apologizing to everyone for the inconvenience. I chuckle to myself because I think it's the first time I've heard her say she was sorry.

Finally, they leave, and I pull a chair up beside her bed. She's laying back against the pillows, her hair fanned out around her, and I realize in that moment there isn't a damn thing on this earth that I can deny her.

"How are you feeling?" I ask, setting the bag from the gift shop on the floor at my feet along with the vase of flowers and cactus. She looked at me. Dark circles under her eyes but she couldn't be more beautiful if she tried.

"Tired. I'm sorry Declan for putting you through this."

"Stop apologizing, you have nothing to be sorry for. Now here." I picked up the bag and sat it on my lap. Pulling each item out, I handed it to her. With each item placed in her hands, her eyes brightened a little more.

"And these are for you too." I picked up the plant and flowers and stood up.

Her eyes grew large. "A cactus? You got me a cactus?" she said. Ending the question with a laugh she laid a hand on her right side. "Owww!! God that hurt!"

"I'm sorry, I didn't mean to—"

"Now who is the one that doesn't need to apologize?" she asked with an impish grin.

"You got me there," I said, turning to put the plant on the windowsill.

"Can I see the flowers please?" she asked.

"Of course." I held them out to her so she could look at them. A soft smile on her lips as she tried to lean forward but stopped. "Here." I plucked the only rose in the bunch and held it out for her to take.

I watched in fascination as she brought it to her nose and inhaled deeply. "I've never been given flowers in my life," she whispered as she laid it on her chest and looked at me with complete adoration.

I set the vase beside the cactus and thought if she looked at me like that every time I gave her flowers I would be bringing them to her daily.

Yawning, she said, "You should go home and get some rest."

As much as I hated the thought of leaving her, she was right, I did need to go, but not home to rest.

I pulled my cell phone from my pocket and placed it into her hand. "Yeah, I think you're right. Will you be okay?"

She nodded. "Why are you giving me your cell phone?"

"You don't have one, and all the numbers to reach someone are in the contacts, including the landline for the house. Besides, I have my watch and there's a spare phone in the center console of the Caddy. I'll text you from it when I get to the car."

She shook her head, barely keeping her eyes opened, yet she tried to hand it back to me. "But what if you break down on your way home?" She put her hand to her head. "Oh wait, I'm more tired than I thought. I'm sorry."

"It's fine. Don't worry about it." I leaned down, intending on brushing my lips against her forehead, but instead, I captured her mouth with mine. No tongue, just a chaste kiss that lingered but with a promise of what was to come. When I stood, her lips were still puckered.

"Get some sleep goose, I'll see you in the morning."

I looked back as I came to the door, and she was already asleep.

Once I left the hospital, I called Rory on my watch and asked him where he parked the Caddy and then I told him to meet me down on Yonge Street with some 'tools'.

∞∞∞

After the bait was laid, we sat in the Caddy in wait, and I could feel Rory's eyes on me.

I look at him. "What?"

"It's two in the morning, and I smell like a dirty pussy!" Rory spat. "You're fucking crazy, you know that don't you?"

I laugh. "A little bit."

He gestures towards the dark building. "Taco Bell isn't even open to get a bite to eat."

"Stop your whining and keep your eyes peeled."

He huffs and looks out his window. "What color was it again?"

"Dirty gray, long hair. About yay big." I hold my hands apart showing him an approximate size.

Rory points. "Is that it?"

I lean across the seat and look out his window. "Yup, that's the one. Looks a little smaller than I remember though."

Its nose twitched at the enticing smell of fish. Zeroing in on the scent, it slunk over to the pile of tuna inside the live trap. Before it could take a step inside, another identical kitten darted past it into the trap. We held our breath, waiting for the moment that the trap door would slap down but it didn't.

"Well, what the hell!" Rory laughed. "I swear I tested it before I brought it from the barn."

I sat back in my seat. "What did you test it with?"

"A brick."

I roll my eyes. "For fuck's sake. The kitten doesn't weigh as much as a brick Rory!"

He rubbed his chin. "No. I guess it wouldn't." He turned and looked out his window and grabbed my arm. A bold move if there ever was one. "Look! The other one is going in too."

I shook his arm off and looked out the window too. The first one on the scene took a tentative step inside, sniffing the metal wires as he did, but the scent of the tuna was too much to deny. Another step in, and a shift of its little body as he began to eat, and the trap door shut.

"Wooooo! Yes!" Rory yelled, pounding the ceiling of the car.

"You put a dent in my roof, and I'll kill you." I muttered.

"Oh, fuck off, you know you love me," he grinned. "What are you going to do with two of them? They look like spitfires they do."

I pushed open my door and grabbed the towel that was sitting on the console. "Take them to the Vet. Correction, you're going to take them to the Vet tomorrow while I go visit Wren."

I left the door open and walked over to the trap. I picked it up just as Rory joined me. "I can't take them.

I gotta take my mum tomorrow to the doctors."

Both kittens looked harmless. Cowering together as far away from me as possible. "Fine. I'll drop them off before going up to see her," I said, poking my finger between the mesh squares. A hiss and a swipe later, I was scratched and bitten. "Little fucker."

"You better get a rabies shot. They could be rabid," Rory said.

I set the trap back on the ground and covered it with the towel. "Do they look rabid? No, they are starving and scared. Come on, let's get out of here."

Walking back to the Caddy, I opened the back passenger seat and placed the cage in a way that it was wedged between the front seat and the back. Unless I rolled the car, it wasn't going anywhere.

Rory was standing there looking at his phone. "There's a twenty four hour Vet down the street about a block away. Why don't you just take them there? Also see if you should get a rabies shot," he chuckled.

"Yeah. That's a good idea." I rub my chin. "But I don't want to leave Wren alone. I don't trust McLean not to find out she's here."

"Take them. I'll go keep watch outside her door," Rory offered.

"What about taking your mother in the morning?"

"Won't be the first time I lost sleep," he laughed and waved as he headed towards his vehicle, and I went to get in behind the wheel of the Caddy and stopped.

"Rory."

He froze mid step and looked at me. "Yeah boss?"

"Thanks. For everything."

The look on his face you would have thought I gave him a million bucks.

"My pleasure. I'll see you when you get back to the hospital."

Nodding, I got in, started the vehicle, and pulled out of the parking lot and headed to the Veterinarian clinic.

Chapter 18

Wren

The next time I open my eyes dawn is just breaking outside my window, and Declan is slouched, asleep in the chair with a laptop open on a nearby table.

A nurse walks in and smiles at me. "Morning Wren, how are you feeling?" she whispers.

"I'm okay. How long has he been sitting there?" I ask, looking at him.

"Oh gee, he came in around 4:30 this morning. Normally we don't allow people to stay with patients, but he was pretty persistent," she smiled. "I'd say he's smitten with you."

I chuckled and immediately regretted it. Wincing, I said, "He does have a commanding personality I have to admit."

She put a blood pressure cuff around my arm and nodded. "He does. You're a very lucky lady."

Lucky? Smitten? I highly doubted it. Not after less than a week of knowing each other. But I had to admit, I was smitten for him and damn lucky that he was the one that almost ran me over.

"When can I leave?" I asked when she took the cuff off my arm, she pushed a button and raised the head of the bed.

"It's up to the doctor, but usually patients are in for a day after an appendectomy."

"Oh fuck," Declan groaned, his voice raspy with sleep. He then sat up and stretched and both of us watched as the material of his shirt lay taut against the muscles of his chest.

The nurse bit her lower lip and muttered, "You're a very lucky woman indeed." She shook herself as if she were in a trance, looked at me and cheerfully said, "Your breakfast will be here shortly." Then she quickly left the room.

"Morning," he said, coming to sit on the edge of the bed as he wiped the sleep from his eyes. "How are you feeling?"

"Better. Not nearly in as much pain when you brought me here." I move my hands to try to scooch up, but Declan sprang to action. Stuffing his hands under my armpits he hiked me up like I weighed nothing.

"Better?" he asked, looking down at me.

I nod and mumble my thanks. His nearness has my pulse racing. I can feel it, but he can hear it. The damn machine monitoring my heart rate starts beeping like crazy, and the nurse comes back into the room.

"Oh… it's just you," she says, giving Declan a

dazzling smile and a bashful wave before leaving the room.

"I think she likes you," I said, feeling the green-eyed monster rearing its ugly head. The woman was gorgeous.

"Maybe." He shrugged a shoulder as he sat back down on the bed. "I don't care if she does. I'm only interested in you."

For a minute I thought he was falling for me, and I was elated, I think. Or it could have just been gas because I felt a bubble rise from my belly.

But then he swallowed hard, like he tasted something vile and finished by saying, "and your well being."

"Oh... well that's nice." I smoothed the blanket under my palms and smiled at him. A fake smile of course because what the hell was I to do?

"Here is your food!" A staff member from the kitchen came in carrying a tray.

Declan stood up and pulled a bed tray over. "You eat, I'm going to see when I can take you home."

It turned out he could take me home as soon as the surgeon came in to check on me. Because now we are just pulling into the circular driveway out front of his home.

"Don't you dare open that door," he said to me as he turned the Caddy off. He opened his door and hurried around to my side, flinging my door wide.

Leaning forward, he unbuckled my seat belt and lifted me out of the car. There was no use arguing with him that I could walk. I tried that at the hospital. One look at him told me otherwise. I think he just likes lugging my ass around just to get a workout in.

He turns around and heads towards the front door, and it suddenly opens to see Connor standing there.

"You gave me quite the fright last night," he said, smiling at me.

I laughed. "Sorry for telling you off. I didn't mean that."

He laughed as he headed off towards the kitchen. "Yes, you did."

"Declan, you can put me down now," I said, a grin on my lips from the banter with Connor.

He sighed, like he was tired of hearing that. "I will, on the sofa."

He walked right to the living room off the dining room and set me down on my feet right in front of the couch.

"Sit," he ordered.

I didn't think twice, my legs felt like jelly. Carefully, as if I were a plank of wood, I flopped into the soft leather and was promptly covered with the softest blanket my skin ever had the pleasure of feeling.

I smiled up at Declan. "Thank you."

"Don't mention it. I'll be right back."

I watched him walk into the dining room and disappear into the kitchen. Bored out of my mind, my eyes were drawn to the fire snapping in the hearth and that's when I noticed a TV above it. That wasn't there before. I glanced around looking for the remote control and noticed a romance novel on the coffee table. One that I hadn't read yet. If I leaned a certain way, I may just be able to reach it.

I slumped to the left and stuck my hand out, my fingertips waggling in the air, trying to grasp it.

"What the hell are you doing, goose?"

I quickly tried to sit straight and instantly regretted it. "Ouch!" I put my palm against the bandage and sat there half ass.

"That will teach you! When the doctor said not to move, he meant it." He came around the back of the couch and set a steaming cup of tea beside the book, then hiked me up into a better position.

"I was just trying to get the book." I mumbled, feeling like a chastised child as the doorbell rang.

"Don't move," he warned, and went to answer it.

I huffed and bit my thumb nail. If Declan was going to coddle me for a week, it may just drive me crazy. But as he walked back, carrying a box, with a sexy as hell grin on his face, the idea of being coddled sounded delightful, as long as he wasn't scowling at me.

He set the box on my lap. "That's for you."

"Oh, my clothes!" I said, looking at it.

"Maybe." He took a metal object from his back pocket, flipped it around in his hand and handed me the handle of a knife. "Open it."

Startled at his theatrics with the blade, I took it from him and said, ""Oh! What the heck kind of knife is that?! Can you teach me how to do that?"

He laughed. "We'll see. And it's a butterfly knife, totally illegal to have."

"I'm okay with that," I said, slicing the tape on the box. Handing it back to him, I pulled the flaps open and looked inside. Without saying a word, I looked back up at him and stared. Finally, I said, "These aren't clothes."

"I know." Sitting on the coffee table, he reached in and pulled out a bottle of multivitamins and sat them beside me on the couch. One by one, he pulled a bottle out, and as he did, he said, "Mike suggested that there are supplements that can help with your PCOS. So, I did a little research last night while you were sleeping and ordered everything that was suggested."

Tears spring to my eyes as I gaze at the bottles. I always knew there were supplements that could help but could never afford the cost of them. "Thank you," I whispered as I dashed a tear away and looked at him.

"Do you want this yet?" Connor said, from behind me.

Declan looked at him and shook his head. "I'll let you know."

"Your tux for the swearing in came earlier this morning, by the way," Connor said. I looked at him then, and he hurriedly put his hands behind his back before backstepping to the dining room. He was acting decidedly odd but that flew out of my mind the second his words registered.

I looked at Declan. "Oh my gosh, isn't that tonight?!" What a fricken time to have surgery. After all he had done for me, the one thing he wanted was me to be there and I couldn't. I mean I would go, come hell or high water, but I knew he would refuse.

He shook his head. "It's been postponed until after your recovery."

Relieved that I hadn't ruined it for him I asked, "Can you do that?"

"I can do anything I want."

He stood up from the coffee table and walked to the dining room. Some cussing ensued and I craned my neck to see what all the fuss was about. And in comes Declan walking back into the living room holding a kitten at arm's length around its chest. The kitten from the Taco Bell parking lot.

"Oh my God Declan. You went and got her!!" I squealed like a little girl and took the poor thing, cuddling it in my arms. Looking up at him I say, "Is she for me?"

He nods. "She is."

"But you hate cats."

"Yep, I do… but you don't…"— he pulls his other

arm from behind his back, holding an identical kitten to the one in my arms— "…there were two of them. I didn't know which one it was that we saw so I brought both home."

This time when the tears sprang to my eyes, they fell like a waterfall.

Chapter 19

Declan

It's been a fuck of a week spending every waking hour with Wren. Not because she's annoying, quite the opposite. She's funny as hell, and a quick study. Learning the trick to make a butterfly knife open as graceful as she has is no easy feat. But she conquered it. She even managed somehow to mend the hard feelings I've harbored against my father. Helping me to understand his newly diagnosed Dementia and what not to say or do to make his reactions worse.

No. It's been pure hell because every time I'm near her, I want to pound her into next Tuesday. Standing at the door of our adjoining bathroom, like a fucking creeper, watching her sleep while I jerk off has been helpful, but not enough. Her scent is driving me insane. And the thought of planting myself between her thighs makes my hips start to gyrate on their own for fuck's sake. I believe in being a clean man but taking five cold showers a day is getting to be a bit much.

Rubbing the stubble on my chin I watch as she sits

on the library floor, hair still damp from her shower, leaning forward, playing with the kittens. It gives a good vantage of her cleavage, and I want to bury my face between her tits.

"How are you feeling?" I ask, wishing I hadn't because she sits up, her eyes bright, with a smile on her face and my free peep show is gone.

"I told you two days ago I'm fine. I wish you would stop worrying about me."

"Yeah. I know." I cough. "That dress fits you well."

"Thanks. I think." She squints at me. "Is there something wrong with you?"

Do I tell her? Yeah, I've had a hard on since the second I met you! No, that would be admitting she has a power over me that even I can't control.

"No. Nothing is wrong." I shake my head. Connor steps into the room and announces he is taking my dad to his weekly visit at the Alzheimer's Society. Something my dad looks forward to.

"Grab a pizza for dinner on your way home," I say to Connor.

"The usual?" he asks.

"That and a few pounds of wings too. Wren, is there anything you want?" I ask, looking at her.

"Cheesy bread?"

I nod. "Add two orders of cheesy bread."

"Will do! See you in a couple of hours." We both watch Connor leave the room and I slink down on the floor with her.

"Want to play a game?" I ask.

"Sure, what kind of game? Poker or blackjack?" she asks, moving to stand to get the deck of cards. Something we've done for the past week to pass the time.

I grab hold of her arm, stopping her and lean close. My voice comes out husky as I say, "Hide the weenie."

She laughs. "What the fuck did you just say?"

"You heard me." I wag my eyebrows at her.

She grins. "You're pulling my leg…" She looks at me, and I see the second she realizes that I'm dead serious.

She leans forward and our mouths devour each other's hungrily, and finally, I have her in my arms with an empty house. But then she pulls back.

"Who are you kidding?" she murmurs. "We both know it's more a sausage than a weenie."

I growl as I capture her mouth again and my hands roam over her body. Finding the buttons of her dress at her breasts, I work each one, tugging it free until she's barred from the waist up except her bra.

I drag my mouth from hers and trail it down to the swell of her bosom, her nipples teasing me as they rise and duck behind the lacy material with every rapid breath she takes. Pulling the strap from her shoulders, I don't stop until they are down her arms, and her breasts are free. I sit there a moment, my eyes feasting on her. For once she seems shy as she presses her arms close to her sides, trying to cover herself.

I shake my head. "Don't do that."

She swallows hard. The tip of her tongue darts out to the corner of her swollen lips. "Do what?"

"Try to hide yourself from me."

Wren

"I… I was always teased in high school because of how big my boobs are, how big I am."

God that was hard to admit. But with him staring at me like I was some goddess I felt confident in telling him.

"Oh, I'll tease you alright. I'll worship those pink nipples of yours like they are made of gold." He growled, as he leaned forward and tugged one between his teeth. And just like that, I'm soaking my underwear as his tongue swirls on my breast. I shove my hands in his hair, holding him to me as he sucks in long drawn-out tugs.

I feel his hand slip under the skirt of my dress, smoothing a path up the inside of my thigh, and I spread my legs wide. He drags his thumb across the material covering my pussy. I hate that word. I've always associated that word with being sexual or sensual, something I never felt with the one man I'd been with before, my ex. He was always slam bam thank you ma'am only he never thanked me. But that was until now, and that's exactly what it was. A pussy dripping with sexual anticipation for him.

I begin to whimper as he digs his fingers in the waistband of my underwear and lifts my butt off the floor, helping him along. Pulling them off, he buries his face in them and inhales sharply.

"I'll be keeping these," he murmurs, tossing them aside.

I almost burst out laughing because this hot as fuck Mafia dude wants to keep my underwear. *To sniff.*

A bubble of laughter is threatening to escape past my lips until he ducks under my skirt, and I immediately tamp it down. I have never had the pleasure of experiencing this and I'm not sure if I want to. But then his hot breath fans against my skin, and I can't lay back on the floor fast enough.

"Wait," I say, tapping him on the head. I look down the length of myself to see his head bob up under my skirt.

"What for?" he pushes my dress off his head and looks at me.

Still not entirely sure how I will react and needing a distraction, I say, "I think if you're insisting on doing this, that I should do the same for you."

"Insisting? If you don't want to do…"—He stares at me for a second and then his eyes darken— "wait… you want to do a 69?"

Biting my lip I nod. "Yeah. I've never done it before."

His eyes darken. "Are you sure? Your side—"

"Is fine, I've been cleared for all normal activities,

remember?"

"There's nothing normal about what I want to do to you, little Goose."

His voice is a growl that sends heat pooling low in my belly. "Show me."

For a moment, he's perfectly still, searching my face. Then something snaps and he's off the floor and standing there with his hand held out to me. "Fucking right I'll show you but were going to my room."

His enthusiasm has me laughing when I say, "I have a bed in my room, you know. It's closer."

He gives me a quick nod, as a wicked smile curves his lips. "But I have a mirror. I want you to see what I see," he murmurs, as he plays with my hair. "I want you to watch while I take you apart."

I take his hand, and he pulls me to my feet. Never letting go of it, he stoops to snag my underwear from the floor, and he leads the way to his bedroom.

Declan

The second the door closes, we are stripping one another's clothes off until we both stand naked, and I worry for a moment if my dick is going to choose at this moment to deflate like a balloon. Only one way to find out.

"C'mere." I reach around to the back of her neck and pull her to me until her breasts are pressed flat against my chest. So far so good. The feel of her nipples pressing against me is the stimulation that I need.

My mouth finds hers and our tongues tangle as I reach around to her ass, hiking her even tighter against me. I gyrate my hips, grinding my cock against her.

Squatting, I slide my hands to the backs of her thighs and pick her up. She lets out a little whoop of surprise as I carry her to my bed. She's dripping on my dick, and I want nothing more than to fill her void with one thrust, but I know she will scream in agony.

Instead, I sit on the side of the bed and lay down, pulling her on top.

"Declan, I should be on the bottom," she mutters, sliding off me.

"Absolutely not. I'd crush you. Not to mention choke you with my dick." As long as it stays stiff as a board I silently add. I shake my head, and spin around, facing her feet. "You're going to be the one in control of how far you take me in."

"Fine." She sighs and climbs on top. A minute goes by and then I feel her begin to stroke my penis. Not being able to wait a second longer, I nuzzle her pussy lips wide with my tongue and plunge it inside.

I'm rewarded with a groan as she takes me into her mouth, and I want to ram my hips upward, forcing more down her throat, but the urge to cause her no harm is stronger than my carnal need. This isn't just about me, but for her too.

Nibbling on her clit, I slide one finger inside her slick heavenly sweetness, followed by another. I start to fingerfuck her as I lap up her juices, and I can feel her starting to lose momentum.

"You can take it baby." I murmur, urging her on, and she begins to match me stroke for stroke.

I can feel the veins in my neck start to bulge, the more I fight it the worse it is. Almost painful in a way and I wait until we both have climbed to that precipice that we've been striving for. We freeze at the same time, feeling the same thing. A void of everything but each other. Like entering an abyss only for it to end in an earth shattering burst of starlight.

"Well, that was gross." She slides off me, and we both lay there catching our breath. "I don't mind giving you head, but I will never swallow that again."

I laugh as I trail my fingers along her hip. "Salty, was it?"

"Yeah. The time back at the restaurant I'd just eaten a mozzarella stick and thought it was that. Clearly it wasn't. I once read where eating pineapple would help. You should probably try that. So, you ready for round two?"

I shook my head at her jumping from one topic to another and just answered her. "Are you?"

She sits up and smiles at me. "Yes, as much as I enjoyed it, I think I'd like to know what it feels like to ride your dick."

I wrinkle my brow. Should I tell her before I met her

what it was like?

"Sorry I... was that too much?"

"No, it's fine." I sit up, long enough to switch positions, then pull her down beside me, to lay face to face. "I wasn't going to tell you this, but the night at the restaurant..." I stop almost afraid to admit that I, a man in his prime, have been dealing with erectile dysfunction for the last 12 months. What if it turned her off?

"What is it? Did you steal my boots?"

A bark of laughter escapes me. Leave it to her to say something like that and ease my tension.

"No," I shake my head. "That night was the first time I had a hard on in over a year, and it was because of you. And since that day, all I can think about is fucking you." There I said it. I admitted she has a hold on me.

She closes her eyes like she's not quite sure she heard me right, then opens them looking me straight in the eyes and says, "You had a limp dick for a year? I bet you didn't go to a doctor for it either!"

I laugh. "Yeah, I guess you could put it that way, and no, I didn't." I pulled her close until our noses touched. "Thank you for bringing it back to life."

She kissed me so softly that my head spun. But then I could taste the saltiness of her tears as she took my face in her hands and whispered, "You're welcome."

My thumb found her nipple, and it sprang into a stiff peak under my touch. "I know you're not a virgin," I murmured. "But you're tight as fuck, and I'm going to enjoy every second stretching that pussy of yours."

"I'll accept that challenge!" she smiled as I dipped my head, claiming her nipple with my teeth. Soothing the sting away with my tongue, I slipped my hand between us to the junction of her thighs finding her clit. Wedging my knee between her thighs, she opened her legs, and I slipped a finger inside, then dragging it up to rub her clit.

Jerky sensations ran along her body as I played with it, making her body sing.

When I stopped, she cried out as I knelt between her legs.

"Wait!" She put her hand on my chest, and I frowned, wondering if she was having second thoughts. But she surprised me when she flipped onto her stomach. Her eyes met mine in the mirrored headboard as she stuck her ass up in the air. "Take me now!"

I laughed, thinking gladly. "Are you sure? It's gonna be deep."

"Yesss," she hissed. "I'm sure."

"You better grab hold of that bar on the headboard then."

She gripped it till her knuckles turned white, waiting for me to make a move, and when I did, she jerked.

"Is it going to rip me open?" she asked, hesitantly.

"No." I splayed my hand on the small of her back. "Just relax, you're already too tight. And so you know, I'll pull out just before I go off."

The second I eased into her silkiness, I could feel her insides accommodating my girth. "You're doing good baby, just a little bit more," I hissed, ready to explode inside her.

Sweat beaded on her skin as her head dropped down.

"Look at me Wren. Eyes on me," I ground out as I filled her to the hilt and forced myself to hold still. Letting her get accustomed to me, was close to my undoing.

Her head snapped up and our eyes met in the mirror. "That's it little goose, watch me. Don't think of anything else, the pain will pass. I promise."

I slowly started backing out, her muscles clenching around me as if trying to capture every inch of my shaft. She backed up a notch, the tip of my dick was so sensitive at this point that if she moved one second more, I would be going off. I planted my hands on her hips and held her right there as I held back with every ounce of restraint I possessed.

When it passed, I met her gaze in the mirror. "Not so fast." Easing forward I slid my length back inside her, and this time when I pulled out, I reached around and found her clit.

A cry erupted from her lips, not of pain but of pleasure, and I knew she was ready. I started to pump my hips against her, the sound of skin slapping together filled the room. It felt so fucking good as the walls of her vagina clamped around me with every outward stroke, like they were trying to absorb my dick, and I was losing all control. Darkness started to take over my vision, and before I knew it, stars started shooting behind my closed eyes. There was no way I could pull out like I had told her. With one last final thrust, I shot every one of my swimmers into her succulent pussy.

Wren

For several minutes, we lie in silence, our heartbeats gradually slowing. His fingers trace lazy patterns on my back, and I feel myself drifting toward sleep when his voice pulls me back.

"Are you okay?" he asks, lifting my chin to search my face.

"More than okay," I assure him, pressing a kiss to his jaw. "That was..."

"Fucking awesome." he finishes, a hint of worry creasing his brow. "Wasn't it?"

I smile, snuggling closer. "In the best way."

The worry eases from his expression, replaced by a satisfaction that makes my heart flutter. He pulls the blanket over us, tucking it around my shoulders before his arm settles around my waist, drawing me against the solid warmth of his body.

Outside, the storm continues to rage, rain lashing

against the windows and thunder rumbling in the distance. But here, in the circle of Declan's arms, I feel safer than I've ever been.

As I drift toward sleep, I realize with startling clarity that I'm falling for him, fast. The thought should terrify me—this dangerous man with his weapons room and his enemies—but instead, it feels like coming home.

"Declan?" I murmur, already half-asleep.

"Hmm?" His fingers continue their gentle path along my spine.

"Thank you for the kittens."

His chest rumbles with silent laughter. "Go to sleep, little Goose."

Chapter 20

Wren

It was the night of Declan's swearing in, and I felt like throwing up. Not because I was sick but from nerves. A room full of mafia men was unnerving enough but just the thought of having all those judging eyes on me because I would be by Declan's side was the cause of it.

The only thing that is calming my stomach down is thinking about him. The day we finally did the deed was magical in more ways than one. Not only did it feel incredible, but it also brought Declan and I closer together.

The past week, we have spent time in each others' arms. Sleeping together in his bed and exploring each other's bodies in ways that I never knew existed, and I'm happy to report he is one solid man. I don't know if I will ever get used to the look of carnal lust coming from his eyes every time he looks at me. Like he's doing now as I fluff my hair for the tenth time.

He came up behind me and laid his hands on my shoulders. Bending down he nuzzled my neck and murmured, "Goose, you look gorgeous. We're going to be late if you don't stop playing with your hair."

"Okay, okay I know! I just don't want to embarrass you is all." I said, trying to pull the sweetheart neckline of my jumpsuit higher. The bra that Janice picked out from the shop fit perfectly but not so perfectly because it barely covered the dusky part of my nipples. If it weren't for the fuzzy edging along the neckline, everyone would be getting a show.

His hands slip to my waist and turn me away from the mirror, and I pucker my lips at him waiting for a kiss.

"I'm not going to kiss you because if I do, we will never leave." He pushes me past him and smacks me on the ass. "That's a reminder for what's to come later. When we get home, I'm going to enjoy stripping that jumpsuit off you."

I giggle as I gather my clutch and slip on my heels, and he holds my coat from me to put on. Donning it, I button it up and tie the belt around my waist as tight as I can stand it. Maybe it will keep the vomit in check. "Okay, I'm ready."

Declan

I love watching her walk outside to the Caddy. Ever since we left the bedroom, my eyes have been glued to her ass. I want nothing more than to forget about this evening and stay wrapped in one another's arms. But I can't delay the swearing in a day longer. Word has it that if I don't take control now, someone else will do it for me. Someone in the family. If that weren't bad enough, I'm dealing with McLean and his men creeping around our estate. Ever since I left him that little note via his son, he's been scoping out the estate, gearing up to take it over. How, with only ten men? Well, nine actually, since one took a bullet between the eyes. I have no clue, but he's welcome to try.

As I help Wren into the Caddy, I scope the area, making sure my men are in their spots. Wren, none the wiser, chatters on about throwing up.

Wren

Declan pulls the Caddy onto a long tree lined driveway. Lamp posts guide our way in the night to what looks to be a country club in the middle of nowhere. After sucking on a peppermint, he handed me, the nausea subsided, and I gawked in wonder at the stately home made of white sandstone, set in the near distance.

"What is this place?" I ask, as he slowly makes his way up the drive.

"This is Highland Hills. A private golf club for the family."

The nervousness that I had been feeling before

was nothing compared to now, not after seeing the number of cars parked in the parking lot. "How big is your family?" I whisper, my eyes staring at the sea of expensive automobiles.

"Ah, a few hundred members. Not that many compared to other organizations." He reached across and took my hand in his. "You will be fine."

I look at him and say, "I suppose you can't just link the swearing in on YouTube huh?"

He burst out laughing as he pulled up in front of the doors of a stately looking building.

"Yeah, no that's not going to happen," he said, shaking his head as the valet opened our doors. Declan got out and came to my side of the vehicle and took my hand in his.

Swallowing the bile that started to rise I grabbed onto his hand for dear life. "I'm just going to find a corner and sit in it, okay?"

He laughed. "You will sit by my side."

He pulled me along until we entered through the wooden double doors, and a man stood there, offering to take my coat.

"I'm good." I shook my head. "I'll just keep it on."

"Wren, take your coat off," Declan murmured out the side of his mouth as he handed his coat to the awaiting man.

Reluctantly, I undid the belt and buttons and slid the coat off me. A tug of war ensued with the doorman until Declan offered me his arm. Together we walked into a room that was set up with row upon row of chairs, only they weren't empty. All eyes turned on us as we walked up the middle aisle to a stage. Declan showed me to a chair, right beside Connor, who grabbed my hand and plunked me onto it. He leaned towards me. "You're doing great. You look smashing."

I smiled at him. Then I turned my attention to Declan. If anyone looked smashing it was him in his black tuxedo, I thought as he walked out of the room. "Where is he going?"

"Oh, he's meeting up with Tomas and Rory. They will come out together shortly on the stage."

"Oh." I sat there a moment in silence then said, "Do you think Tomas will remember what he has to say?"

Connor nodded. "He's been practicing all week. Let's just hope he keeps his skirt down and doesn't show his ass to everyone."

I whipped my head around to look at him. "What?! Did you just say a skirt?"

He shrugged. "Well, a kilt is what it is. They're in a state of nature under them, you know. Anyway, that's where they all went. They went to change."

My brows shot skyward. "A state of nature?"

"Naked Wren, they're naked as a jaybird under their kilts."

My eyes bug out of my head as a soft, "Oh," escaped past my lips.

He laughs at me as a commotion off stage could be heard.

"I can do it myself goddammit!" Tomas marches across the stage with Declan and Rory a step behind him, tugging the back of his kilt down.

He smacks their hands away and takes a step towards the microphone attached to a podium and starts talking.

I don't hear a damn word coming out of that man's mouth because I'm staring at Declan, and I start to feel a tightness between my legs. I bite my lip while squeezing my knees together and take the sight of him all in.

He's wearing a black short coat with silver buttons, over a black vest and white shirt. A navy-blue tie around his neck, matches the main color of his kilt. But it's his socks that catch my attention the most, encasing his calf muscles to just below his knees. Which draws my eye upwards, to the skin above and the start of his muscular thighs. It stopped there because the kilt covered them. But I found as I hunkered down into my seat, I could see more of his powerful thighs, and I wished I had my moisture wicking underwear on, heck even a pad would work. Thank God the chairs were covered with a dark cloth and not vinyl. I sunk just a tad lower as I was sure any minute now, I would be seeing his—

A loud cough next to me snaps me out of my peep show, and I shoot Connor an annoying glance, before looking away guiltily right at Declan's face.

A grin spreads across his lips as he shoots me a wink and for some dumb reason I start to blush profusely. I need a distraction and dart my gaze to Rory, which really doesn't help. He stands next to Declan in his Irish finery, and if I didn't have my heart set on Declan, I would definitely hit that up. Especially with his dark hair, hanging over his forehead, giving him an almost rakish appearance, to me he was a man of mystery.

Sitting up in my seat, I realize that not a single word coming from Tomas' lips is registering in my head. "What is he saying?"

Connor chuckled softly. "It's old Gaelic. Don't worry about it, half the room won't understand it either."

I nodded and watched as he waved his hands over cloth draped over the podium, then he took a long-handled knife from a table. I held my breath as he took his son's hand in his and pricked his finger with the tip of the blade. Squeezing a few drops of Declan's blood onto the cloth he said a few words, and Declan repeated it back. From what I gathered, that was the oath Declan just swore to.

When Tomas was done, he picked up the cloth and draped it over Declan's left shoulder. I looked around as people started to stand and clap.

I pulled on Connor's sleeve. "What's going on now?"

"Stand up and clap."

I immediately did so and looked up at Declan. He was staring right at me with a smile on his face. I stood there still clapping and felt a tug on my arm. It was Connor. "What?" I asked, looking down at him.

"Sit down. It's Rory's turn to be sworn in."

I glanced around the room to see all eyes on me because I was the only one still standing clapping. So much for not wanting to draw attention to myself. I sat quickly and didn't move a muscle as Declan started Rory's swearing in.

I felt like I was at a wedding reception and he and I were the bride and groom. Instead of having bride's maids, I had henchmen. Not just henchmen. Declan's chosen. The ones that, no matter what happens, will have his back.

I leaned towards Declan. "Are we expected to eat all of this?"

All of *this* was a feast set before us on the main table and everyone else sitting at the round tables had to stand in line at the smorgasbord to wait their turn.

He leans down our shoulders rubbing and whispers in my ear, "Eat as much as you want, you're going to need it."

I look him in the eyes, wondering what he meant by that. "For?"

"Stamina." He winks at me. Then with a grin on his face he grabs the turkey leg off his plate, and I watch as he takes a healthy bite. He reminds me of a king back in the day, and it hits me. He embodies the essence of a bygone king—a ruler who feasted with primal gusto, his courtiers watching in awe. Only it's me that is gawking in awe, and for a second, it terrifies me. Because in that second is when I realize that I'm falling in love with Declan.

The tables are pushed back from the center of the floor and the staff is cleaning up any spilled food in preparation for dancing. And I'm sitting on a chair, stuffed from that fantastic food, in the corner watching as everyone converges on Declan, giving him their well wishes.

The first few notes of Lily-Rose Depp's sultry voice play out of the sound system. The Void, one of my favorite songs of hers, grows in tempo, and Declan starts to look around the room. His eyes darken as they settle on me, and I shiver, knowing he is undressing me with that look.

"Dance with me." His voice, velvety yet raspy has me creaming without hesitation as I take his hand and I allow him to guide me to the dance floor. He pulls me close, so close that my boobs are close to popping out of my bra, but I don't care because I'm where I feel the safest, in his arms.

As I rest my head against his chest and listen to his heartbeat accelerate, neither of us say a word as we sway to the music. We don't need to because our bodies are conversing. His hard shaft, rubbing against me with every step, has had me in a perpetual state of wetness since the second I saw him in his kilt. My nipples poking into his chest like spears is a testament to that, and I can't wait to get home with him. That is until he pulls back.

"What do you want?"

I pop my head off his shoulder, confused by the anger in his voice and look directly into the eyes of an ice queen. A bitchy looking one.

Chapter 21

Declan

I stare into the eyes of Gretchen Callaway. My ex, and wondered what the hell I ever saw in her. Superficially she was stunning. Inside, she was a cold, manipulative, heartless narcissistic bitch. The epitome of a gaslighter if I ever did see one and her arctic gaze has settled on Wren.

Taking her hand, I tuck her behind me and look at the bane of my existence. "What do you want, Gretchen?"

A sneer erupts on her lips. "You certainly downgraded, didn't you Declan."

I feel Wren squeeze my hand, then she lets go of it and steps beside me. She looks Gretchen up and down.

As tears gathered in her eyes, she wiped them away and rather loudly, muttered, "At least my tits are real." Then she spins on her heel and runs from the scene.

I watch her and take note of which door she escaped out of before turning my gaze onto the bitch. "Rory."

He moves to stand beside me. His gaze never

wavering from her face, he says, "Yeah boss?"

"Get rid of this trash, will you?"

Knowing exactly what I meant by the term, Gretchen's eyes grow large as my words sink in and Rory grabs her by the arm.

She shakes her head in denial. "I… I didn't mean anything by it, Declan. I was just jealous. I'm still in love with you! Please don't do this!"

Ignoring her struggle, Rory looks at me over the top of her head. "Where shall I dump it sir?"

"The usual. The waterfront."

He nods and drags a very unwilling Gretchen away to meet her maker, and I head in the direction that Wren took off.

Wren

I lean against the cement railing of the patio as tears stream down my face replaying what just happened over and over in my mind. I was momentarily stunned seeing Gretchen standing before Declan. Truth be told, I thought maybe she was his cousin at first. An annoying one but the second she opened her mouth and said downgraded, I knew she was his ex-girlfriend, and my heart dropped to the floor. She was back in his life. There was not one flaw on her slim, big, bosomed body and there was no way I could compete with that. Nor would I want to.

I suck in a shaky breath and cast my eyes on the moon and say, "Oh well, it was good while it lasted."

"It isn't over," he murmurs next to my ear and turns me around to face him. Raising his hand, he drags his thumbs over my tear-stained cheeks then takes my face in his hands. "Unlike you little goose, she meant nothing to me."

I open my mouth to call him a bald-faced liar, but he puts his finger over my lips, smooshing them closed.

"Shh. I'm not finished," he murmured. He took a shaky breath in, like he was scared of what he was about to say.

"I know when it's my time to meet my maker, I will never get into heaven for the deeds I've done," — he takes my chin in his hand and tilts it towards him and stares intently into my eyes — "and I don't care because every second I'm with you, I'm already there."

Speechless, I stood there staring at him as he took my hand. "C'mon, let's get out of here."

That snapped me out of my daze as he dragged me along. Digging my heels in I said, "Wait a minute. Did you just confess that you love me?"

He stopped and looked off into the darkness, and I wished I could read his mind.

Finally, after a solid minute, I know because I counted the seconds it took him to answer, he turned his gaze on me.

"I strongly like you."

I couldn't help it, but I had to ask. "Stronger than Gretchen?"

He laughed as he gathered me close. "A thousand times stronger than her. C'mon, let's go home."

Declan

On the way home she can't keep her hands off me. Stroking my thigh, her hand slips under my kilt and starts caressing my balls.

"Fuck it!" I growled, pulling off into a rest stop. The second I throw the gear shift into park; Wren is tearing her seat belt off and launching herself at me. I hit the power seat button and move it back as far as it will go as she yanks up my kilt and takes my dick between her lips. Her tugging it into her mouth has me almost creaming into her throat. Almost. As much as I love her sucking on my cock, this is not the place for it as cars zip by. I pull her up and onto my lap and start to devour her mouth as my dick bobs against her warmth, threatening to poke a hole in her clothes as she straddles my thighs.

In a flash, my tongue is tickling her tonsils as I pull her coat from her shoulders. Dragging my mouth away from her luscious lips, I plant it on her bare shoulders, trailing a path down to the swell of her breast as she rocks against my cock. She leans back against the steering wheel as she pops open her bra and hits the horn. She jerks against me in alarm, and her hot snatch rubs against my throbbing dick once more.

She giggles and flattens herself against my chest. "That scared the hell out of me," she said, catching her breath. "How far away are we from the house?"

"Ten minutes. Why?"

She crawls off me and flops into her seat. "Because I'm wearing a fucking jumpsuit! Get home!"

I laugh as I put my seat back into position and pull the kilt back into place. "Eager, are you?"

She nods, the tip of her tongue runs along her top lip. "You could say that."

I put the car into gear and step on the accelerator. With every mile I drive, Wren's hand is stroking my dick, and I fight not to explode. We make it back to the house in five minutes.

I pull the Caddy into the garage and cut the engine and we both exit leaving our doors open. Rounding the hood, right into each other's arms, our mouths clash as we tear at each other's clothes, until she's standing in nothing but a bra and me with the front of my kilt tucked into the waistband. I lift her by the hips and set her on the hood of the Caddy. I drag two cinder blocks over and stand on them, hoping I don't tip off, I yank her to the edge of the hood. She cries out, wrapping her legs around my hips as I slide into her slick pussy. I lick her cleavage and bite her breast, leaving my mark on her as I pump my hips. The only sound in the garage is skin slapping against skin and her moaning. We are both close to going off until the sound of a car coming up the drive has me ducking, looking through the windshield through to the back window at a set of headlights in the dark.

I freeze. "Fuck! Hang on, goose." She looks at me dazed as I tap my watch.

"Nooo, please don't stop!" she pleads. Then she starts to pump her hips up and down in long slow strokes, taking me all in like a wicked dance of sin and I know she's going over the edge. But I can't just yet. I clench my teeth so hard a muscle starts to jump along my jawline. My balls are ready to blow, but I'll be damned if I'll do it in front of an audience.

The speakers in the car connect as I call Connor. The person who is driving the car with my father in the passenger seat. And in less than a minute they will be pulling into the garage, right beside the Caddy. That's not going to happen. Wren starts moaning loudly as he picks up and I reach for her bra strap yanking it down, rolling her nipple between my thumb and index finger as she shudders her release.

"Boss? Is that you?" Connor's concerned voice echoes through the garage.

"Yeah. Stop that damn car," I grunt as I smack my hips against her. Pushing her legs to the sides, I grind into her flesh, as deep as I can go.

"Is everything okay?" Connor asks.

I glance up to see him still coming, at a faster pace I

might add, and Wren begins to shudder and scream a second time. This time the walls of her vagina squeeze tight around my shaft, and I'm losing the battle.

"Connor," I snarl. "If you don't stop that fucking car now, I will personally feed you to the fish."

The car stops about 500 feet away, and I disconnect the call just in time too. I can't hold it a second longer and as I start to go off, I tug her nipple between my lips, sucking on it for all it's worth as I spill my load into her.

I collapse against her for a second, forgetting all about my father and Connor waiting to come into the garage.

Wren taps me on the shoulder. "You can put me down now."

Not moving a muscle, I raise my head and look at her. "That's the first time I've ever done that."

She looks at me confused. "Done what?"

"Held back from going off and not lost an erection." I let go of her legs as I step off the cinder blocks and shove them out of the way so she can slide down the front of the car.

She slips her coat over her nakedness and picks up her clothes, "Have you ever made a woman orgasm twice in one go around?"

I looked at her for a full ten seconds, while I untucked my kilt. then grinned. "No, I can't say that I have."

She giggles and grabs me by my tie and tugs. "Come

on stud, you can gloat in the bedroom while we go at it again. Oh, and you better let Connor know he's safe to come in now."

We are laying in my bed. Her head is resting on my chest, and I smooth my jaw over the softness of her hair as she delicately snores, exhausted from having multiple orgasms, I suppose. And I did that. To think that four months ago I couldn't get a hard on if my life depended on it and now, the woman in my arms fixed that.

I let out a soft satisfied sigh and pulled her tighter to me. If it were any other woman, I would be nuts to even think this. But not Wren.

Closing my eyes, I settle down to get some sleep. Tomorrow was going to be a busy day.

Chapter 22

Wren

I wake up to the weight of Declan's leg across my thigh, his arm thrown across my waist, my nose buried against his chest. I take in a lungful of air and inhale his manly scent. I snuggle closer to him and then it hits me. My bladder has other ideas. Carefully, I untangle myself from his limbs and slink off the bed to the bathroom. Still groggy with sleep, I plop onto the throne and do my business.

Once done, I move to the sink and become painfully aware of every joint in my body. I smile. Last night's love making was one for the books that was for sure. Washing my hands, I look at myself in the mirror and see the bite marks left by Declan. The memory of his teeth on my skin sends a shiver down my spine as I head back to the bedroom.

I stop in the doorway and look at his smooth skin, taut over his muscles even in sleep, and I want to go over and lick him awake. But I don't. He needs his rest. I know this because many a night I've awakened to find him sitting in the chair by the window. Watching the night.

He's worried about something, likely the fact there's still a hit on both our heads, at least I assume there was because that was well over a month ago and not one attempt has been made. Personally, I think it was all talk. No one would be so stupid to take on Declan and his family.

I turn around and head back through the bathroom to my bedroom in search of clothes. I'm still not comfortable enough to walk around the house in just a robe, not when Connor and his father are around at least.

I pull out a pair of underwear and a bra from the dresser drawer and toss them on my bed, followed by a pair of sweatpants and a t-shirt. I quickly dress then step into my slippers before pulling on a zip up hoodie. Running a brush through my hair, I pull it back into a low ponytail and head out into the hallway.

The smell of bacon hits me as I head towards the stairs, and I follow the scent all the way to the kitchen.

"Morning Wren, how did you sleep?" Connor smiles at me as he sets a steaming cup of coffee before me.

I have to wonder if he figured out what Declan and I had been up to in the garage last night. Hoping he didn't, I took a gulp of the brew before answering.

"Peaceful," I said. "What are you cooking there?"

"A bit of everything." He spooned some fluffy scrambled eggs onto an awaiting plate, added a few slices of bacon and two slices of toast. Setting it before me, he smirked, "I figured you and Declan would need a hearty meal after last night."

Good lord he knew.

I scrubbed a hand down my face, as he pushed a bowl of freshly sliced fruit my way and topped it all off with a glass of orange juice.

"You dig in now. I'm going to head up and take Tomas a tray."

I nodded and picked up my fork. I watched him load the tray as I stabbed a strawberry and popped it into my mouth. It wasn't until he picked up the tray that I dug into my food like a ravenous animal. I hated to admit it, but Connor was right, after last night, the food definitely hit the spot.

"There you are," Declan said, coming into the kitchen. He went directly to the coffee machine and poured himself a cup. "You left before I woke up."

I stood and collected my dishes. "You were sleeping so soundly that I didn't want to wake you." Walking over to the sink, I looked at him over my shoulder as I rinsed them and said, "Take a seat, I'll get you some food."

He shook his head then looked at his watch. "Can't I have to head into the city in a few minutes."

As I loaded the dishes into the dishwasher, I found it odd that he didn't ask me to come with him. Which was fine, it's not like we needed to spend every second of the day together. But a niggling started in my brain. He was going to see Gretchen.

I squint at him, folding my arms across my chest.

"What?" He raises his brows and sets his mug on the countertop.

"Where did you say you were going?"

He snagged a slice of bacon out of the frying pan then kissed me on the lips.

Never taking his eyes from mine, he took a bite of the meat, slowly chewed it then swallowed. "I didn't." Turning on his heel, he waved as he headed towards the mudroom and the garage. "I'll see you after lunch."

I stood there long after he'd disappeared around the corner. Contemplating my options. I could leave and head back to my apartment. That was if I still had one or I could go to my father. Something that I did not want to do.

Sighing I pushed away from the counter and headed into the living room. It was time that I lost myself in that romance book that had been sitting on the coffee table ever since I got out of the hospital.

Declan

I knew from the look on her face she suspected that something was up. Good, because there was. I pull into a parking space outside of the Jackson's tack shop and turn the Caddy off. Wren doesn't know it yet, but a young mare is being delivered just for her, and I'm here to pick up a few things for it.

Getting out of the car, I lock it and make my way to the entrance. Standing behind the counter with his back to me, is the only man that I trust to take care of my horses. He was also the only friend I had when I'd come back to live with my father. Jackson turns around and a grin splits his face.

"How the hell are you Declan?" He comes from around the counter and gives me a bear hug.

I smack him on the back. "Good. How are things with you?"

"Oh, you know, same old same old." He went around the counter and bent down to retrieve a box. Setting it on the counter he removed a smaller box and handed it to me. "Please don't tell me you named a horse this?"

I chuckled as I took it from him. Opening the box, I traced my thumb over the words *Little Goose*, written backwards on the branding iron and said, "No. I gave a woman that nickname."

He burst out laughing. "And she still talks to you?"

I smiled and nodded as I reached for my wallet. "Surprisingly, yes."

Jackson started to ring up my order and shook his head. "Leave it to you to come up with a name like that."

I pulled out my debit card and tapped the machine "Yeah, well it's a fitting name. She's a squawker." I put the iron in the larger box and lifted it off the counter. "When will you have some free time? I'll need you to come out for a fitting for a custom saddle."

"Does it mean I get to meet little goose?"

I laughed. "It does. The saddle is for her and the horse that is being delivered this afternoon."

Pen in hand, Jackson looked at his appointment book. "How's Saturday around 2pm?"

"Works for me."

"Good. You take care and I'll see you Saturday."

As I headed across the sidewalk out to the Caddy a black SUV was coming up the street. Call it intuition but the second the window started to roll down, I made a beeline for my vehicle. The sound of bullets ricocheting off the buildings reached my ears long before the SUV was even with me. Novices. It gave me the chance to take cover behind the Caddy as the SUV sped past.

I unlocked the Caddy and tossed the box into the back seat then went around and got in. Starting it, I cranked the steering wheel and made a U-turn in the middle of the street. The idiots were so new at this that they had kept driving down the street instead of trying to evade being caught. Amateurs.

Fumbling in the center console, I stepped on the gas, and pulled alongside of them. Rolling the passenger window down, I racked the slide of my Glock and raised my hand and fired. The bullet punched a nice clean hole through the window before it found its new home in the Driver's temple.

I cranked the steering wheel hard to the left and sped down a narrow street. The sound of cars crashing could be heard in my wake. Taking the next right, I head to the end of the street where one of our warehouses sits. It's armed to the tits, cameras everywhere and an alarm that goes straight to my phone if someone feels the need to break in. I pull up to the gate and punch in the code. With a creak, the rusty gates swing open, and I drive inside of the yard. On a timer, they close behind me, and I pull the Caddy behind a brick wall, completely hidden from the street. I turn it off and get out, locking it behind me as I reach a door. I hold my hand against the palm scanner and hear the click of the door unlocking.

Pulling out my cellphone as I push the door open, I call the house. Connor answers it on the second ring.

"What's up, Declan?"

I feel for the light switch and flick it on. And there she is, sitting under the lights, the last gift my mother ever gave me. A Jaguar Project 8; a monster of a car. Sleek, elegant, and never driven.

"Everything alright at home?" I ask.

"Yeah. We were just playing a game of crokinole. Man, those checkers hurt when you flick them with your nail."

I chuckle. Leave it to Connor to go off topic. "Keep an eye out, would you? McLean's men shot at me as I was leaving the tack store."

"You were just—"

"Don't tell them. Just keep an eye out, I'll be home soon."

"Okay, I'll do that."

We end the call, and I walk around the car. A fine layer of dust covers it, and I walk over to a faucet on the far wall that has a garden hose attached to it. A quick rinse and I'll switch it out for the Caddy. Not ideal considering there is still salt on the roads from the last snowfall, but there isn't a doubt in my mind that the cops would be searching for it.

Chapter 23

Wren

Eyes glued to my book, I reach for my cup and take a sip of tea, immediately spitting it back into the mug. It's cold.

Setting it back on the table, I look at the kittens laying atop the blanket covering my legs. I hate to disturb the little ones, but I need to go to the bathroom. Carefully, I pull myself out from under it, barely disturbing them, and head off to the washroom down the hall.

Connor stops me in the hallway. "I was coming to find you. Tomas wants to know if you want to play a game of Yahtzee?"

I dance on the spot. The need to pee is stronger now that I'm standing outside the washroom. "Ah...Yeah, sure that sounds like fun. Are you two down in the basement?"

He nods. "I'm just heading to the kitchen to get refreshments. Want anything?"

I slap my hand on the door, hoping he takes that hint that this is not the time for a chit chat. "Whatever you guys are having sounds divine."

"But you don't know what we are having."

I reach for the button on my jeans and start to undo them. "Connor! I'm about to piss myself. Get me whatever you want."

I push my way into the bathroom and slam the door. Making it to the toilet just in time. As I sit there, relief washes over me, but it's short lived when I hear a loud bang alongside the outside wall. Quickly I finish up and make my way over to the window. I can't see anything. I hurry out into the hallway and make my way towards the kitchen. Connor is looking out the patio doors towards the barn.

"What the hell was that?" I ask as I move to stand beside him to look out the window, and I freeze.

The barn is on fire and horses are running wild. "Oh my god!" Grabbing his arm, I start to tug him towards the door. "We need to help them!"

He takes hold of my arm and steers me away. "We can't. I need to get you and Tomas into the panic room, now."

I dig in my heels and spin around to look at him. "The panic room?! Why? It's a barn fire and those horses need our help!"

"Wren, that isn't just a fire. We are under attack. Now come on," he said, tugging me along through the hall to the basement stairs.

"Wait!! I need to get the kittens."

I take off running to the sofa where I'd left them

and breathe a sigh of relief, they are still there. Snatching them up, I hurry back to Connor, and we make our way downstairs, to see Tomas sitting there, rolling the dice from the Yahtzee game.

"Attack?" I whispered to Connor. "Who is attacking us?"

"McLean's gang. They've been snooping around for a few weeks." He moves over to where Tomas is sitting and takes the old man gently by the arm. "Come on Tomas, we are going to play this in the hidden rooms."

Tomas looks up with confusion in his eyes. "The hidden rooms?"

"Mhm. Wren, can you open the door please?" Connor asks, gathering the game under one arm and guiding Tomas out of his chair.

A loud bang reverberates on the ceiling, and Connor says, "Hurry now, Wren."

I jump at his request and head to the open doorway with the bookshelf. I slid the picture aside and stared at the keypad. What the hell was the code again?

Putting a hand to my head I closed my eyes. Declan's' soothing voice echoed through my mind *'The code is 719290, in case I'm not here and you need to get inside.'*

Wishing he were beside me, I quickly punched in the numbers and the door to the right slid open revealing the steel door. I put the code in a second time, and it seamlessly slid open.

Unlike the day Declan showed me the panic rooms,

the gun cases were closed. Their wooden panels hide them from view. Where was that switch to open them again? I would figure it out later, for now, Tomas and Connor needed to be secured in the rooms.

Stepping aside I thrust the kittens into Tomas's arms and held the door open for them to enter.

"Close the door, Wren." Connor said, guiding Tomas to a table.

I shook my head and took a step back. "I can't do that. It's my fault this is happening."

"Wren, get the hell in here now! Declan will kill me if anything happens to you."

Tears sprang to my eyes as I said, "I'll leave him a note."

I jumped back over the threshold as he started towards me. "Tell Declan that I love him, will you? Goodbye, Connor."

"You can't—" I smacked the switch on the panel and the door slammed shut, cutting off his words.

I took a deep breath and wiped the tears from my eyes then started searching for the button to open the gun panels. It's not like I knew how to shoot a gun, but I could at least try.

The sound of glass shattering from the bar area tells me that I don't have time to look for the hidden buttons. I glance around the small room and spy a candelabra sitting on a table. A sob escapes past my lips. I was joking the day we were in the room about my weapon of choice, evidently, he took me seriously.

Snatching it up, I head out to the bookcase and hit the red button before sliding the picture back in place then crouched down in the corner.

I wasn't going to just go out like a mad woman brandishing my candle holder. I mean they might not even look in here. But I was wrong.

A bottle was thrown at the bookcase, and I breathed a sigh of relief when the photo came away unscathed. I couldn't let them find that panel. A delayed reaction if there ever was one, I opened my mouth and let out a scream and cowered in the corner like the scared woman they were expecting.

Footsteps hurried over to my hiding spot, and I heard a man say, "I found her boss. What do you want me to do with her?"

The crackling sound from a walkie talkie filled the little room as a voice said, "Bring her to me."

Hands grabbed a hold of me under my arms and the next thing I know I'm being hoisted off the floor. I recognized him from the night I'd escaped from the church. Swinging with all my might, I whack him across the face with the candleholder.

As he drops me and begins to howl, I dart past him right into the chest of his partner. I grab a hold of his arm as he shoves me back and the gold bracelet he was wearing, I unclasp it, without his knowledge. As he raises his arm, I cringe knowing he's going to backhand me. Without a second thought, I drop my hands and let the bracelet slip to the floor hoping that it goes unnoticed by him just as his hand connects with my jaw. I drop like a brick, the last thing on my mind before darkness hits me is Declan.

Declan

Pointing down at the glass display counter in front of me and saying, "Let me see that one."

I watch as the middle-aged woman bends down and pulls the tray out just far enough to make my selection. "This one?" she asks, her hand hovering.

"Yes."

She shoves the tray back and stands straight. "Sir, that's an eighty-thousand-dollar ring."

I raise a brow at her. Judgemental much?

Leaning on the counter I glance at her name tag. "Vera. Did I ask you about the price tag? No. Now you can either let me see the ring, or I can take my business elsewhere."

A man older than Vera moseys on over and sets her aside. "Ignore my wife. Which ring was it?"

A smile tugs at the corner of my lips as Vera tsks and sets off to dust a plant. "The pear shaped one. Is it platinum or white gold?"

"You guessed it right the first time." He bends to retrieve the tray and sets it on the display counter for me. "It's platinum."

I pick it up and look at the stones' brilliant shine. "What's the grade of the diamond?"

He hands me a jeweler's loupe and reads off the particulars about it from its certificate as I look through the glass. It's a gorgeous stone and perfect for Wren.

I handed the ring back to him. "I'll take it."

The man grins like its Christmas morning and says, "Is it the proper size or will you need it adjusted?"

"Good question." I frown. I didn't know her finger size. "I'll give you a call if it does."

"Certainly." He took a box from underneath and placed the ring inside, snapping it closed, he placed it into a larger hinged box and nested it inside then closed the lid. "How did you want to pay for it?"

I reached in my back pocket and pulled my wallet out. Taking the black card from its slot, I handed it to him. His brows rose in surprise, but he didn't say a word. As the transaction was processed, he pulled out a bag and placed the box inside. "Whoever you bought that for must be one special lady."

I stuffed it back into my wallet and smiled as my phone began to ring. "She is," I said as I pulled the cellphone from my pocket. "Excuse me for a minute."

He nodded, and I turned my back on him to answer the call.

"What is it?" I said into the mic.

"Mr. Declan?"

I squint at the sound of a kid's voice coming over the wire.

"Who is this?" I bark.

"It's Ian, the stable hand. They set the barn on fire and..."

I broke out in a cold sweat as his words sunk in, and I started making my way to the door. "And what?"

"Sir you're bag?"

I stopped at the jeweler's voice and turned. "Put it in the safe, I'll be back for it."

I pushed the door open and headed to the Jag. Clenching my phone, I said, "And what Ian?"

The barn was set up with a sprinkler system and would put out any fire. The horses would go crazy, but they would be fine. I prayed he would just say they got out and were running around the fields, but God doesn't answer the prayers of sinners.

The blood in my veins turned to ice when he muttered, "And the house."

"Where is Wren and my father?" I demanded.

Swallowing the sting of tears lodged in my throat, I jumped in the car and started the engine. The call connected to the Bluetooth, and I could hear the shake in Ian's voice when he said, "I... I don't know sir, I haven't seen—"

A muffling sound came over the speakers as I zipped through the streets.

"Declan, it's Connor."

The air rushed out of my lungs as I exhaled. "Thank fucking God. Is everyone okay?"

"Yeah, your dad remembered the tunnel going to the guard shack."

I wiped a hand down my face. "Good. Let me talk to Wren."

"Um…"

My mouth suddenly went as dry as the desert. I should have known something was up from the way he was talking but it never dawned on me until he said that one word.

"Don't you dare!" Tears started streaming down my face. "Don't you dare fucking tell me they took her Connor."

As I drove out of the woods and saw the estate below, I realized that my world was on fire and the one person that would have made a difference in what I was feeling, was gone. Taken, against her will. McLean doesn't realize it yet, but he was a dead man.

Chapter 24

Wren

I feel the gentle rocking of a vehicle driving down a dirt road, and I'm transported back in time.

To a time when I was laying in the back of my father's car as we headed home from a family night at the local drive in. I look to the front passenger seat, and I can see my mother sitting there glancing at my dad with a smile on her face.

Those were happy times, until his drinking and gambling got in the way, and my mother decided to leave us. I never understood why she would leave me with an alcoholic who had a gambling problem. It's not like I was a mouthy kid, quite the opposite. Her leaving me forced me to become the person I am. Which is exactly what I need at the moment.

My tongue goes to the corner of my lips, and I taste blood as I run it along the seam. The right side is noticeably bigger and all I can think of is 'great, my second fat lip in less than six months'. I open my eyes and try to focus on the man sitting in the passenger seat. Was he one of the guys from the church? I couldn't be certain, and it didn't matter. Right now, I needed to come up with a plan to get the hell out of the car.

I wiggle my feet and find them loose. Good, at least I will be able to run when the need arises. Now if I could only somehow loosen the duct tape around my wrist. I bend my fingers, feeling for the end of the tape but stop when I hear the man in the driver seat speak.

"When I came to work for McLean this wasn't part of the deal, Cookie," he grumbled to the driver.

"You think I like this any better than you? After what he did to McLean's son, I don't want no part of this. I worked for Declan, or did you forget? Once he finds out that we have his woman, he's going to come for us."

So many thoughts were running through my head. Like why the hell did a full-grown man have a name like Cookie? And I liked the sound of me being referred to as 'his woman', but I couldn't help but wonder what Declan had done to McLean's son. Whatever it was, he never mentioned it to me.

I darted my eyes to the man in the passenger seat and saw the fear on his face. "Why don't we just drop her off on the side of the road then?"

I pull myself to a sitting position and stick my face between the front seats. "Yes, why don't you? By the way, what did Declan do to McLean's son?"

They both scream like the little girls that they are, and I say, "Come on now. You knew I was back here, you put me here!"

A call comes over the speakers before they can respond and with a shaky finger, the passenger accepts the call.

"Where the hell are you?" A voice barks out over the speakers that I can only presume to be McLean.

"Hey boss, we are ten minutes out," Cookie, the driver, said.

"That's ten minutes too long. Haul ass. And did you find Gretchen at the MacGallan estate? She hasn't been home since the night of his swearing in."

My brows rise so high that I can feel them disappear behind my bangs. Who the hell was Gretchen to McLean?

"I swear to God that if he harmed one hair on my daughter's head, I'll slice every one of Wren's fingers off with a laser before I kill her."

"Geezus," Cookie mumbles under his breath as McLean disconnects the call. His hands tighten on the steering wheel as he swings his gaze to look at me. "Did you see Gretchen at the swearing in?"

I shake my head as I lean back against the seat. "No. Never heard that name before."

As the car speeds down the road to my fate, I forget all about escaping. I can't help but sit there in stunned silence and wonder how Declan never knew that Gretchen was McLean's daughter.

Declan

Twenty-four hours ago, I was buying Wren a ring, and now I sit here sifting through the wreckage of my house. Having sent Connor and my father to a hotel in T.O. I'm here alone. Luckily the fire only reached as far as the kitchen and garage before the fire department got it under control and the barn's sprinkler system stopped it from reaching past the tack shop.

I've been up all night, looking for any sign of who did this, and for the life of me, I can't figure it out. My mind screams that it's McLean, but it was executed so skillfully that I'm having doubts because everywhere that I look is destroyed. Glass lay strewn upon the floors from broken windows and furniture slashed open, the stuffing tossed at will. It's as if they were looking for something other than revenge.

I head down into the basement and see every bottle from the bar smashed on the floor. The slate on the pool table, shattered and yet none of it bothers me until I make my way to where the bookcase is with the hidden panel. My blood begins to boil when I spot the candelabra laying on the ground and I see red when my eyes go to the blood splatter on the wall. That could only mean one thing, Wren put up a fight trying to protect the panic rooms.

I bend down to pick up the last thing she touched, the candle holder, when I see a flash just under the bookshelf. Leaning forward, I reach under and pull out a thick gold chain. It's a bracelet, and I know at once it doesn't belong to anyone here. Not with the name *Cookie* engraved on it. My fingers close around it and squeeze as if whoever the owner is could feel my hand around their neck as I choke the life force out of them.

Standing up, I set the candelabra on the bookshelf and pull out my cellphone to call Rory. He picks up on the first ring.

"Sir, tell me what you need," he says in a way of greeting.

"I need you to find out who Cookie is. And Rory, find out fast because I'm going out hunting."

We end the call at that, and I head back upstairs to find the fire inspector standing in the middle of what was the kitchen.

He turns at the sound of my footsteps, and I meet my cousin Cillian's eyes. "Declan man, I'm sorry," he said. "Who the fuck did this to you and Uncle Tomas?"

I nod. "Thanks, and I have a pretty good idea who did it," I said as I looked around at the charred kitchen cupboards. The only thing not destroyed was the countertops, but I wouldn't trust them to not shatter. They will have to go.

Cillian nods as he looks around. "The garage is a write off too. Lucky for you the barn didn't sustain too much damage other than smoke."

I lean a hand on the countertop. "I figured as much.

How long is this going to take?"

"An arson investigation can take upwards of six months with—"

I cut him off with a shake of my head. "Not happening. My father needs his house."

Cillian leaned his hands on the counter and stared right at me. "I know, but the insurance company will want a full investigation."

"Fuck the insurance company, I'll pay out of pocket and have a new garage and kitchen in less than a month."

I was mildly surprised when he agreed with me. "I'll file it under accidental. But keep your mouth shut about it or it's my ass."

I laughed for the first time since Ian called me yesterday afternoon, but it wasn't a laugh of mirth, it was a laugh of a maniacal man instead. "No worries there, buddy."

My phone started ringing, and I glanced at my watch. It was Rory. Not wanting to seem rude I ignored it, but Cillian told me to go ahead and that he was heading out.

With a wave to him, I answered the phone. "Talk to me, man."

"Word on the street is that 'Cookie' is none other than Liam McCrae."

"Thanks Rory. Now find out where McLean is holed up," I said, before hanging up the phone.

Fuck, a Scotsman. He wasn't loyal to the Irish mob;

he was only loyal to the highest payer. I know because he was one of the men standing on the edge of the forest the night I found Wren. The same man that used to work for me, who now worked for McLean. I should have killed him when he left, but I felt sorry for the man having to support his grandfather, his only living relative. But then again if I had, I wouldn't know who has her, at least now I had a lead.

Turning on my heel, I head out to the front foyer and out to my car. Getting in, I start it and the engine roars to life. The rumble that reverberates throughout the car soothes me. Soon I will be heading on the road with the beast, and nothing will stop me until I find Wren.

But not until I hear back from Rory. For the first time in my life, I'm at a loss as to what to do so I drive the car over to the barn and see Jasper standing there in the pasture looking forlorn. The sight of the majestic horse pulls at my heartstrings. I shut the car off and get out then walk over to him. Reaching out I rub his neck and talk in hushed tones. It takes him a full minute before he realizes that it's me, and he nuzzles my hair like he always has. I give him a gentle push and say, "Meet me inside boy."

I watch as he does what I ask as I make my way back to the car and drive up to the barn doors.

Getting out, I pull the tack box from the back seat and go inside the barn. Jasper is waiting for me in the hallway as I set it down on the wooden plank floor, and I unhook the barn doors and slide them open.

Pulling out the little fire pit for branding I set it aflame with a torch. Before placing the iron that I had made for Wren close to the flames, I screwed a handle onto it, and set it along the edge, close enough for it to get hot. Walking over to a cabinet hung on the wall, I pull the doors open and toss things aside until I find what I'm looking for. As I walk back to the pit to add my find to the flames, I look at Jasper, "Are you hungry boy?"

He gives me a whinny and a nod of his head. A genuine smile spreads upon my lips while I walk over to the feed bin to grab a scoop of grain. Dumping it into the bucket in his stall, I pat his neck as he passes by me then I head back out to the fire pit.

The flames have died down and the coals are glowing red, as red as the sun going down outside the barn doors. I lean against the doorway and wonder where I will even begin to start looking for Wren. My first guess is the seedy underground. The strip clubs. I pray Rory has a narrowed down list soon.

But while I wait for word on where to begin, I need to do something. Pushing away from the door frame I head over to where the riding crops are. Taking one off a hook, I put it between my teeth and pull a stool close to the fire pit. My hands reach for the buckle of my belt and as I undo it, I watch the coals. Mesmerized by their glow, I can't help but wonder if Wren is cold or hungry or if she's even alive.

I undo the button of my jeans followed by the zipper and tug them and my boxers down around my hips. Jasper is watching me as I pick up the branding iron for Wren. Biting down hard on the crop, I place the red-hot steel against my skin a couple of inches above my dick. Sweat pours out of me as I hold it there to the count of ten and the scent of burnt flesh fills my nostrils. Tossing it into a nearby water bucket, I glance at the horse as I reach for the second one for a repeat. It feels like his wise eyes are judging me, or maybe he just knows I'm not in a good mental state. Either way, I press the second iron to my skin and almost pass out from the flash of white-hot fire cooking my skin.

Tossing it too into the bucket of water, I stand and move to the cabinet, taking out a jar of salve. Unscrewing the lid, I dip my fingers inside and smooth a generous amount onto the burns before pulling my boxers up. I slide my jeans back up, wincing as the rough denim brushes against the still-tender skin. The burn wasn't just about the pain—it was a promise. A permanent reminder etched into my flesh that I would find her, no matter what it took. Wren belongs to me, and McLean is going to learn that the hard way.

I grab my phone and call Rory back.

"I need everything we have on Liam McCrae," I say, the instant he picks up. "His address, known associates, favorite haunts—anything."

"Already on it," Rory replies. "What about his grandfather?"

I pause, considering. "Him too. If McCrae's still supporting him, we might have leverage."

"You going to use an old man to get to him?"

My jaw clenches. "I'm going to do whatever it takes to get Wren back."

The line goes quiet for a moment. "I'll send what I find but it won't likely be anytime soon. I would suggest you get some rest. But knowing you, you won't. Just don't do anything stupid before backup arrives."

I hung up without promising anything. Stupid is relative when the woman you love has been taken.

Jasper huffs from his stall, pawing at the ground. "I know, boy I've gone crazy. I can't help it."

I take out the branding irons from the bucket and set them on a shelf to dry then dump the water on the coals.

Jasper is watching my every move now, and as I make my way over to his stall, he whinnies. Rory was right, I need sleep.

"Care for a sleepover?" I ask him as I take the saddle blanket hanging on a nail and shake it out.

As if he remembers all the nights we slept outside under the stars, he lays down waiting for me to spread the blanket on the ground because he knows that I will rest my head on his neck.

I do just that. Lay the blanket on the ground and curl up on my side. With his neck as my pillow, I fall asleep almost instantly from exhaustion, knowing that the sentinel beast beneath me has my back.

It felt like I'd just fallen asleep when my phone

buzzed with an incoming text. I was shocked to see four hours had passed when I read the message.

An address from Rory—the grandfather is dead, but there is a bar, the 'Cherry Pit'. Good ole Finnigan Green the fine proprietor of the shitty establishment may have information about Wren. At least that's the word on the street. It's not much, but it's a start. I grab my jacket and keys, then pause at the cabinet, reaching for the gun I keep inside. The weight of it feels right in my hand, familiar and deadly.

"Hang on, Wren," I whisper to the empty barn. "I'm coming for you."

As I step out into the night, I know one thing for certain—Oscar McLean is going to wish he'd never heard my name.

Chapter 25

Wren

We pull onto a long driveway with an old farmhouse at the end of it. And for some reason I feel like I've been there before, but I can't place when. Maybe I dreamt it, I don't know. But one thing I do know is I don't want to go inside.

"Come on girlie," Cookie says to me as he pulls me from the car. "Time to meet the boss man. The one that would have been your father-in-law."

I never thought of that, and I feel the need to vomit. This guy must be a real treat to have Gretchen and what's his name, my intended, as children. I stumble up the steps of the porch, if it weren't for the two goons holding me by the arms, I'd have fallen on my face.

Cookie lets go of my arm and unlocks the door. Pushing it wide he grins and says, "After you my dear."

I spit in his face as I pass over the threshold, and he shoves me through the foyer into a living room with a fire roaring in the fireplace. This time when I stumble, I land hard on my bound wrists.

"Get up!" a voice commands from one of the wingback chairs.

Tears spring to my eyes as I push myself up to my knees, but I refuse to cry. Refuse to show any kind of weakness. Wiping my eyes on my sleeve, I climb to my feet as a man stands up from a chair. I watch as he moves around it to face me, a man in an expensive, impeccable suit, and I almost burst out laughing because I'm staring at a dead ringer of my father.

Wait. It *is* my father.

"*Dad?*"

"Hello Wren."

He's the bossman??? Everything flashes through my mind. The wedding to worm lips, Gretchen being his daughter…

"What the *fuck* is going on? Who are you? Who am I?!" I started sputtering, I couldn't help it. "You have some explaining to do. Now!"

He comes towards me with his palms raised. And in that condescending voice he so favors when talking to me, he says, "Wren, relax."

I hated it when he talked like that to me. I hated him.

"Untie me!" I demanded, thrusting my arms at him.

He shook his head. "That I can't do."

"What?" I spit out. "Fine, I'll do it myself." I brought my wrists to my mouth and started gnashing my teeth at the duct tape.

"Wren, control yourself!" he said, taking me by the arm and shaking me like a wet rag. He steered me over to one of the wingback chairs and pushed me down in one.

I watched as he moved to the other chair and sat down. Leaning forward, he clasped his hands together and looked at me. "I can't untie you because I need you to stay put this time."

I got an uneasy feeling the second he said it. "What do you mean 'this time'?"

I glowered at him as he squirmed in his chair and that's when it hit me. His perfectly styled hair, the suit, the house that we were currently sitting in.

"There never was a gambling debt, was there dad?"

He leaned back in the chair and looked at me. "Oh, there was a debt, but that was paid off a long time ago. Before you were even born." He grabbed the arms of the chair and stood up. Walking to a mini bar, he poured himself a drink. The chinking of the tumbler on the glass brings back a flood of memories to me. Memories that I had buried deep within the recess of my mind. Locked away forever until now.

It was so long ago, the night that my mother left. I was five years old, and we were in this very house, visiting my grandparents on Christmas Eve. I was upstairs sleeping when I heard the glass shatter against my wall. Bolting up in my bed, I pressed my ear to the adjoining wall and heard my parents arguing.

"When did you plan on telling me Dan, if that is

even your name, that you have another wife, another family?!"

"Let it go, it doesn't concern you, Vivienne."

"Like hell it doesn't! Bigamy is illegal in this country!"

"What are you doing? Get back to bed, we will discuss this when we get back home."

"Fuck you! I'm leaving with Wren tonight. You can go back to your other family."

The sound of my mother's screams echoed through my mind, and it's only now that I realize why she wasn't there on Christmas morning. Back then, my dad had said she wasn't feeling well and had gone home. I can still see the worried exchanged glances on my grandparents' faces but neither had questioned their son.

Tears spilling down my cheeks, I look at him. "You killed her, didn't you?"

He spun around and looked at me. "What did you say?"

"You heard me. You killed my mother on Christmas eve because she found out you had another family."

I don't know how he moved so fast but one minute he was by the bar and the next he was snarling in my face. "Shut your mouth, you never could keep your trap shut, could you Wren?"

He should know me better than that. I never did listen to him and couldn't help but twist the knife a little deeper into his gut. "Tell me dad. Why would you cut my fingers off with a laser if Declan did anything to Gretchen? Hmm?"

"What the hell are you talking about? Yes, I had another family, but I was getting a divorce—"

"It was I, Oscar McLean, that will cut your fingers off with a laser. Gretchen is my daughter, and you were to marry my son, Colin, until MacGallan killed him. Now you will marry me."

I turn my eyes to the voice behind me. A man dressed all in black is standing in the doorway. He begins to walk into the room and stares at my father the whole time. As if he's daring him to object.

Frowning, I shake my head. "Declan never killed him. I did. I hit him over the head."

My dad reached out and placed his hand over mine. "No, Wren you didn't. Declan killed him while he was in the hospital, you just put him in a coma."

Refusing to believe that Declan did anything of the sort, I shake my shoulders. "Whatever! I don't care. I'm not marrying anyone. You marry him and if you don't want that, he's just going to have to kill you dad, sorry."

He chuckled like he was expecting I would say that. A tight smile formed on his lips. "Unfortunately for you, it's already been decided."

"Like hell it has!" I stand up, but the sound of a gun cocking coming from behind, has me sitting my ass back down.

"You will do as your father tells you, or I'll have you shot, both of you, right where you sit," McLean said.

If my hands weren't tied, I'd have crossed my arms over my chest and gave him the side eye as I said, "I'm 31. I don't have to listen to my father, or you for that matter. Tell me why you have such a hard on for Declan?"

He smirked. "I'll have fun taming you."

Like hell you will

When I didn't verbally respond to that, he continued. "I believe in no secrets between man and wife, and since you *are* going to be my wife, I'll tell you. Declan broke my daughter's heart when he tossed her to the curb. She came home crying and told me what had happened, and I vowed to get revenge any way I could. Now, with my son dead because of him, and you, being MacGallan's woman, our marriage is the most fitting revenge, don't you think?"

I lifted my chin a notch. "Why don't you just kill him? Wouldn't that be more fitting?"

"Oh no. He can't suffer seeing the woman he loves married to another if he's dead."

His phone starts ringing before I can respond, and I sit there watching him, analyzing him as he listens to the caller. His face takes on a stormy look then suddenly falls. He just got some bad news.

He stuffs the phone in his pocket and without a word withdraws a pocketknife. I can hear my father pleading repeatedly. "Don't do it McLean, don't do it."

The blade flies out and before I know it, he's bending towards me, taking hold of the back of my neck and as he slides the blade into my flesh, he whispers into my ear as a shot rings out. "There will be no wedding after all."

Chapter 26

Declan

I parked the Jag around the back of a building that Rory told me would have some information as to where Wren was being held. That was, if I could find the hidden entry to what he called the pit. A place the owner holed up every night with a few of his cronies' playing cards.

I shot Rory a quick text, telling him to give me a half hour before he entered. Getting out of my car, I grab the Glock from the center counsel and tuck it into the back of my jeans. Pulling my jacket down, I lock the car and walk around to the front doors of the building.

A neon sign flashes 'girls girls girls' repeatedly over a sign that reads 'Cherry Pit', the seediest strip club on Yonge Street.

A brunette beauty standing outside the door, dressed in skimpy clothing looks me up and down and says, "Hey there stud, want to go for a ride?"

I look at her. She's so out of place that I almost laugh in her face. And I need her to get the hell out of here. "I bet you'd like that wouldn't you? Got a smoke?"

I watch as she hurriedly reaches into her purse and pulls out a pack of cigarettes and hands it to me with a lighter.

Watching her the whole time, I make a big production out of pulling one from the pack and hand it back to her. I flick the lighter and cup my hand around the flame. "Nice night for working the corner," I say as I light it. She nods and looks down the street, and I pocket the lighter.

Inhaling the toxic crap into my lungs, I just about choke on it when I say, "What, haven't you met your monthly quota yet for arrests?"

She rolls her eyes and mutters, "Fuck. Am I that obvious?"

"Yeah," I toss the cigarette to the ground and stomp on it. "You might want to move to another area."

She fumbles with the earpiece in her ear and says, "Jimmy, pull the car around. We need to move."

I give her a salute. "You have a nice night out there, officer," I say as I pull open the door and step inside.

The smell of cheap perfume, stale cigarettes and sweat greets my nostrils and it has me gagging, but I force myself to make my way to the bar and take a seat on the only open stool. The topless bartender comes over to me, and I drop a $20 onto the bar and order a beer. In another lifetime I would have been ogling her assets, but not since meeting Wren. "Keep the change," I say as she places a bottle down in front of me.

I take a swig from it and scan the patrons. A husband and wife, and a couple of bikers are sitting on stools at the bar as well. There's a group of frat boys down at the drip bar stuffing five-dollar bills into the thong of the stripper on stage. Each vying for her attention. At one of the tables is an old man, a regular I'm guessing, falling asleep in his beer, a few construction workers are sitting at another and two office geeks at a third table. The rest are empty.

I pick up my bottle and make my way over to the old man and pull out a chair closest to the wall. He jerks awake and stares up at me. "Mind if I take a seat I ask?"

"If you buy me a bottle of beer," — he motions to his half-filled glass, — "this watered down shit ain't doing a thing for me."

I chuckle as I wave the waitress over and drop another twenty onto her tray. "Get my friend here…."

"A Molson. Two please." He holds up two arthritic fingers and smiles at me. "Is that alright?"

"Yeah, it's alright." I drop another five onto her tray. When she walks away, I turn back to the old man. "What's your name?"

"Charlie," he says. Pushing the glass of beer to the side, he leans his forearms on the table. "What's your name?"

For a second, I thought about lying to him, but something told me not to. I wanted him to talk. "Declan… MacGallan."

Saying my name worked.

"Wh… what are you doing in here?"

The waitress came back to the table and set his beers in front of him. He started chugging one as I raised a hand when she tried to give me the change. "Keep it," I said, dismissing her.

I look back at Charlie. "You're a regular here, aren't you?"

He nods. "Been coming for twenty years now. Ever since my wife passed away. I just come for the company."

"Right." I nod as I see Rory coming towards us. "I'll just cut to the chase. Do you want a job?"

He almost spits out his beer. "Me?"

I motion for Rory to take a seat. "Yeah. I'll give you a job if you want one."

He looks at Rory then back at me. "Is this a shakedown?"

He got a laugh out of me with that one. "No, I'm serious. You will live at my place. Rory here will set you up, won't you Rory?"

"Anything you say boss."

Charlie sent Rory a quick glance. "What would I have to do?"

I sat there and thought for a moment. Truth be told, I didn't care if the old man wanted a job or not. But I had to get him out of there before hell was set loose on the place. I blame Wren for that, caring for those who needed it the most.

Finally, I said, "Help clean up the mess that was left behind when McLean's men attacked my home."

Charlie looked at me as if he couldn't quite believe what he'd just heard. "Yeah, I can help with that." He nodded as if convincing himself he hadn't just made a deal with the devil.

"Answer this." I leaned towards him and lowered my voice. "Have you ever seen the hidden door to the pit?"

His eyes darted towards the right of the exit. Right where a four foot pillar stood.

"What's in that pillar?" I asked.

He shrugged. "I don't know. I just know people go in and out of it."

"It has to be a staircase," Rory said, glancing up towards the ceiling.

I raised my bottle to my lips and took a swallow. "Charlie, how do people get in? Is there a hidden lever?"

"I think the bartender lets them in. They always go over and talk to her first, and they ain't ordering a drink."

I glance over to the bartender, and she shoots me a wink. Not what I wanted, but I'll use it to my advantage. I push my chair back and grab my beer. "Rory, take him home and give him a room in the barn."

"But I haven't finished my beer!" Charlie cried.

"You can bring it with you," Rory said as I walked away.

I sauntered up to the bar and sat on the barstool I had vacated earlier. "I'll take another," I said, setting the bottle on the bar along with five twenty-dollar bills. At this rate I'd have to stop at an ATM just to get more cash.

Without batting an eye, she takes the bills and stuffs them into the waist of her jeans. Then she twists open the cap on the bottle and holds it out to me until I take it. "What's your name?"

"Jasper," I say, tipping the bottle to my lips.

"Jasper." She rolls it off her tongue like she's tasting my balls. If only she knew it would be horse balls she would be tasting. Then again, she might be into that kind of thing.

Tired of her game already, I set the bottle down and get to the point. "Tell me. How do I get in the pit?"

She grinned. "That'll cost you another hundred."

I sigh, pulling my wallet from my jeans pocket. I pull out all that I have and spread it on top of the bar. A thousand bucks. "You can have all of it on one condition."

She greedily looks at the money then at me. "What's the condition?"

"You open the door to the pit and clear the joint out."

She looks at her watch and shakes her head. "I can't do that. The boss would have my ass if I closed early."

"Okay then," I say, gathering the bills.

She puts her hand on mine. "Wait. It's only ten minutes until last call. Can't you wait?"

Not knowing if Wren is even alive, I shake my head. "No, I can't."

She leans to the side, then quickly pops back up. "Fine, it's unlocked. I'll pull the fire alarm."

I chuckle at her ingenuity and stand up. "Give me fifteen minutes."

She nods. "I can do that. Just push on the panel closest to the exit. It will pop right open. Here." She hands me a block of wood. "Put that in the door, otherwise it will lock you in and the button is under the table where the lard ass sits and then you will never get out, at least not alive."

She really had no idea who she was talking to.

Chapter 27

Declan

I took my time walking over to the pillar and like she said, pushed on the side closest to the exit. A curved door opened, and I slipped inside. Wedging the wood between the door and the jam, I looked up to see a metal spiral staircase rising above. I took the steps two at a time until I reached the top that opened into a hallway. A wall of one-way glass overlooked the whole bar area, and I had to wonder if I was being watched. Of course I was, either at this very wall or a wall of monitors, but I didn't care. Finnigan Green was expecting me, I'm sure.

I follow the hallway to a door that stands open at the end of it. Without so much as a pause in my step, I walk right in to see the man himself. Only he's not alone. A nude girl, no older than 17, with her back to him is bouncing on the fucker's lap. Tears stream down her face as he holds her around the neck. The sight sickens me, and I pull out my gun. Raising my arm right at her, I say, "Get out."

I didn't have to tell her twice. She scurries past me,

and mumbles, "Thank you," under her breath, and I take hold of her arm before she gets too far away and lean close, whispering, "Get out of the building. And don't lock the curved door on your way out."

I turn my attention to that fat sack of shit Finnigan, sitting in the chair with his pants around his knees. "Now, where were we?"

"Please MacGallan, I didn't do anything!" he pleads, raising his hands in the air.

"I beg to differ." A soft pew sound comes from the tip of the silencer. That and his howling as the bullet grazes his fatty calf muscle is the only indication I just shot a round off.

"That was for the girl. Now, tell me where Wren is, and I'll think about letting you live."

Finnigan starts to piss himself and snot runs down his lip as he blubbers, "I don't know!! All I know was there was a hit on your head and hers."

Aiming for a bit of wood that I see between his legs, I let another bullet loose. Wood flies up onto his ball sack, and he bounces in his seat, crying.

"The next one will be in your left nut if you don't start talking."

He holds up his hands as if he's praying. "Wait.... Wait. In my desk, I have a name... of a chef that might know."

Why the fuck would a chef know where Wren might be.

I motion with the gun for him to move. "Try anything and I'll cut your dick off and stuff it down your throat."

In a hurry to please me, he jumps off the chair, tugging his pants up as he heads to his desk. He starts rummaging through the drawers, tossing papers as he goes. "Here!! It's here!" He slaps the paper down on his desk and slides it towards me.

Without taking my eyes off him, I pick up the paper then glance at it quickly. It's a menu for The Starlight, a high-end classy restaurant. "Who is the chef?"

"Uh… the head chef is Scott. He was in here the other day dropping hints about a hit going down at your place." He slumped into his desk chair. "That's all I know, I swear."

I nod. "Right. I'll be on my way now." I take a step back, then stop. "Where is the switch to unlock the door downstairs?"

"Why? You're not stupid enough to let it lock behind you."

I shake my head. "No, I'm not. But your girl there might have. Where is it?"

He raises his arm and points to a photo behind me next to the door.

"Get over here and show me," I say, snagging a bottle of whiskey from a table. Uncapping it, I take a swig.

Without a word he comes around his desk and lifts the photo. "See, it's right there."

"Take the photo down."

He looks at me with brows raised. "What?"

"Take. The. Photo. Down."

He does what he's told and then I shove him back. Back to the chair he'd been sitting on when I walked into the room. Setting the whisky down on the table, I stuff the gun into the waistband of my jeans, then pull zip ties from my pocket.

Finnigan eyes them. "What are those for?"

I hold them up. "These? These are for you. Can't have you pulling a gun on me as I leave, now, can I?"

He shakes his head as I zip his legs to the chair. "I'd never do that to you."

For a second, I believe him and for another second, I almost feel bad for what's about to happen to Finnigan Green. Especially when he just sits there and lets me tie him up. And I almost have a change of heart. Until the scene with the girl pops into my head, and I know damn well she wasn't the first and likely not the youngest either.

Making sure the ties on his hands are snug, I smack him on the shoulder as I stand and say, "Finnigan my man, you should never trust anyone."

Pulling a rag from my jacket pocket I tie it around the neck of the whisky bottle and take one more swig before replacing the cap.

"Wh…"— he swallows so hard I can see his Adam's apple bob up and down — "what are you doing there?"

I ignore him as I pull the cop's lighter from my pocket. Flicking it, I set the flame to the rag.

Sweat starts to roll down his face. "Declan! I told

you where to find Wren!"

I stroke the stubble on my jaw, like I'm contemplating what he just said. "You didn't tell me shit."

"I told you all I know. You said you would let me live if I told you where Wren is!"

"Oh, I'm not killing you... The fire is."

He watches in horror as the bottle flips through the air and smashes on his desk. Flames lick along its surface, alighting the papers he'd tossed there. His screams reverberate against the walls as I turn and head out the door. But just before I leave, I raise the butt of my gun and smash it into the switch for the door downstairs. Just in case he gets free.

I haul ass down the spiral staircase and hope like fuck the girl left the wedge of wood in place. She did. Shoving it wide, I head out the exit and round the building. The back parking lot is aglow from the tiny window upstairs as Finnigan's screams bounce off the buildings around.

I start the Jag and tromp on the gas, racing into the night towards The Starlight.

I pull up out front of the restaurant and see that it's closed. I look at the time on the navigation screen and curse. Of course it is, it's 3 am. I start to pull out of the parking lot, but something occurs to me. Chefs start in the wee hours of the morning prepping food for the day's menu.

Pulling into the parking lot of a hotel, I park the Jag and get out. A warm breeze coming off Lake Ontario is making it unseasonably warm, especially at three in the morning, and I strip my jacket off and toss it onto the seat. Locking the car with the button on the door, instead of the fob, I close it with a soft thud and head along the parking lot to the sidewalk.

Rounding the fence that is separating the two businesses, I make my way towards the back of the restaurant. A kitchen door bangs open, and I duck behind some bushes. A lady comes out, and slams a screen door shut, muttering about the laziness of the night staff and tosses a few garbage bags into the dumpster.

I watch as she pulls a smoke from her apron and lights it, a few minutes later, she walks over to the screened door, and yells, "Scott! Are you coming out for a smoke or what?"

Well what that tells me is, that I have the right place and that Finnigan wasn't lying. God rest his rotten ass soul.

The door flies open and out walks a man in a chef's jacket. He motions with his hand for a smoke as he sets something on the arm of a plastic lawn chair.

"Did you hear about the fire at the MacGallan estate?" she asks, passing him the pack of cigarettes, while she looks at her phone.

He nods, as he pulls a smoke from the pack. "Oh yeah. I knew about it before it even happened. They even took Declan's woman."

I frown. This guy had to be in thick with McLean. When Rory told me that Finnigan might know what happened to Wren it was a big might. With a gun held at his ball sack, if he had known more, he would have said it.

His face lights up when he flicks the lighter and a sick feeling hits me in the gut, like a kick to the balls. He was at my swearing in. He would have witnessed the outburst between Gretchen and me. He was my cousin Scotty, Cillian's kid brother.

"Holy shit, they pulled a woman from the waterfront. Gretchen Callaway, hey isn't that the woman you have the hots for?" She asks, tossing her butt in a coffee can. When he doesn't answer her, she heads towards the door. "Sorry for your loss. I'll start on the marinade for the chicken breasts." She pulls open the screen and disappears inside.

Scotty nods and pulls out his cellphone and a rage overtakes me as I step out of the bushes, headed right for him. Gretchen of all people? Oh, he was thick in it alright. And I just found my mole in the family.

"Hey Scotty. How's it going?"

His head pops up, the glow from his phone shows the look of fear splattered across his face, until I get closer. "Declan? Is that you?"

"It is." I step closer, the urge to wrap my hands

around his neck is so strong that I need to clench my fists to stop myself.

"What are you doing here?"

I stuff my hands in my back pockets and rock on my feet. "Oh, I was out for a stroll and saw you and your friend there having a smoke." A lame excuse if I ever heard one.

His brows raise up. "At three thirty in the morning you're out walking?"

"Yeah, you know with the fire and everything. Working off some steam." I point to the hotel looming behind him. "We are staying there until the house is repaired."

He nods. "Oh. Didn't it burn to the ground?"

I shake my head. "Nope, just the kitchen and garage. Thankfully no one was killed."

"That's good, I suppose."

Thank. Fucking. God. He just gave me a reason to plow my fist into his face.

"What do you mean by '*suppose*'?"

He lifted an indifferent shoulder. "I didn't mean anything by that."

"Oh, I think you did."

In a blink of an eye, I have my hand fisted in his white chef's jacket and shove him against the dumpster, pinning him there with my forearm. "Talk," I spit out between clenched teeth. "Where is she?"

He has the audacity to shake his head. "I... I don't know what you're talking about."

"Fuck off Scotty. I know you know exactly what I'm talking about. Your friend, who is currently frying down at the Cherry Pit, spilled the beans. Where the fuck is Wren?!"

"She's with her father."

"She hates her father, so she didn't go willingly, and she sure as shit didn't go with him. Cookie. You remember Cookie, don't you?" When he nodded, I continued. "Well, he left a little something behind that led me right to you."

His eyes bugged out of his head. "Wh... what was it?"

I sniffed loudly. "Doesn't matter. What matters is you talking. Now!" I snarled.

"You never deserved Gretchen." Tears started streaming down his face. "And now that she's been identified, that means her father knows she's dead. You can kiss your woman goodbye."

His tooth went flying along with a spurt of blood from me smashing my fist into his face. I closed my eyes and slowly counted to ten. "What does her father have to do with this?"

"Her father is McLean you fuck," he said, then spit in my face.

I slammed his head against the dumpster. "If you don't tell me where she is goddammit, I'll kill you!"

"You can't kill me like you did Finnigan because we

are family." He laughed.

I stayed silent as I mulled that over. He was right. I couldn't kill him when I was second in command. What he apparently didn't know was that rule didn't apply to the captain.

"I'll tell you because I know she is already dead, just like Gretchen. They took her to meet her father at her grandparents' farm—ten minutes from your estate, on the fifth concession, with the longest driveway on the road." He sneers. "Isn't that something? She was practically under your nose, and you didn't even know it."

Taking a step back, I took a deep breath, and sat down on the plastic chair, knocking the object to the ground he'd placed on the arm earlier. I looked down to see that it was a meat thermometer.

Shaking my head, I laugh as I pick it up. "You're right—that is something." I stand and face him.

He runs his tongue along the empty socket where his tooth once was, eyeing me sourly.

"There is one thing you're wrong about, though," I say, twirling the thermometer between my fingertips before settling it into the palm of my hand.

"What's that?"

"Rules don't apply to the captain. I'll see you in hell when I get there."

The "oh shit" look in his eyes is priceless when he realizes what I'm about to do. A look that will be frozen there, until he rots away. At least in the remaining one.

He drops like a sack of potatoes as I turn away and retrace my steps. Back in the Jag, I can hear the screams of his sous chef through the closed windows as I drive off.

I bet she wonders how the hell that meat thermometer wound up lodged in his brain.

Chapter 28

Declan

It's been exactly 88 hours since Wren was taken from me, and it's four in the morning as I drive the Jag past the house and park it in front of the barn. My plan was to head right out to the farm where she was, but after discussing it with Rory, it wasn't such a good idea. Not when I couldn't turn the lights off on the Jag. Nothing said 'intruder' like a car racing up a long ass driveway with headlights ablaze.

Getting out, I head to the barn door, and Jasper starts to whinny before I even have it unlocked. Sliding it open I greet him with a question. "Wanna go for a ride?"

He tosses his head as I open the door to his stall and walks out, waiting for me to saddle him up. I make quick work of it because I know every second it takes me is a second that I may be too late to get to Wren. I refuse to think she's anything other than alive.

When he's ready, I climb on top of him and gather the reins. Without any encouragement other than, "Let's go buddy," we are off into the darkness and headed through the fields towards the house Scotty told me about.

Fifteen minutes later, we are making our way up the long driveway. I let him run to his heart's content on the way over here, which half the time was full tilt. But now he needs to cool down despite me wanting to get there as fast as possible.

Instead of urging him on to trot, I take the time to scope out the place. One window is lit on the main floor and two on the second story. I see no movement, but a car parked up beside the house gives me hope that someone is there.

I steer Jasper towards a tall pine and get down off the saddle, tying the reins around the tree. "Stay," I murmured to him and as I ran my hand down his neck, notes of classical music floated in the air.

I climb up the porch steps without so much as a creak. Not that it would matter. The music would drown out any noise, it was so loud. I look through the open window where the light is on to see a man dressed in black is standing beside it, ripping up what looks like paper and tossing it into the flames as he does so.

Was this McLean?

I have no clue what he looks like, and I curse myself out for not being more in the know, like a

Captain should. Oh well, it doesn't matter. He's a dead man anyway. I pull the gun and knife out and slit the screen, thankful that there is nothing below the window for me to trip up on. As the screen yawns open, I step inside and the floor groans under my weight.

The man spins around and looks at me with a gun at his side. "MacGallan, I knew you would come. As a matter of fact, I was playing the music for you. Fitting don't you think? Seeing how you killed my daughter, and I killed Wren. Now, I get to kill you."

Before he could even raise his hand, my knife was buried into his shoulder. Dropping the gun, he howls with pain as I advance on him. I grab the handle of the blade and twist it. "Where the fuck is Wren?"

A maniacal laugh escapes past his lips. "She's upstairs in the attic, chained to the wall. But I wouldn't go up there if I were you. You can smell the stench of death from the bottom step."

Rage consumes me.

Holding onto the knife, I shove the bastard back with my other hand, and he falls to the floor. Kicking his gun away, I bend low and whisper, "I enjoyed killing Gretchen."

Even though my hands were clean from doing that job, seeing the look of agony in his eyes at the mere mention of her name was somewhat satisfying given the circumstances.

Flipping the fucker onto this stomach, I yank up

his pant leg and slice his right Achilles tendon. He screams, but I ignore him as I fling the knife aside. Grabbing onto the waist of his pants and the back of his collar, I lift him off the floor, intending on chucking the fucker right into the fireplace, face first.

But he starts pleading for his life.

I set him back down on the floor and kick him over so I can look the bastard in the eyes.

"You want to save yourself McLean? Tell me what Wren's father has to do with all of this? Why was he so willing to hand over his daughter to your scumbag son? And don't tell me it was because of a gambling debt."

Sobbing, he sits up and reaches for his injured leg, pressing on the wound. "Because Gretchen refused to marry Cookie."

I shook my head. Not that I blamed Gretchen, you could smell the guy ten feet away. But what the fuck did Cookie have to do with this?

Pressing my boot down on top of his left foot, I said, "You need to elaborate."

"Ow, ow ow! Okay, okay, Okay! Wren was Cookie's half sister. Dan, their father, wanted to join forces and thought it best if our kids were married. It would give us more power, he said. When Gretchen refused, Dan offered Wren as a solution and came up with the excuse that I was going to kill him over a gambling debt."

My eyes narrowed at the word 'was'. Wren was

Cookie's half sister. Before, I never quite believed him when he said that little goose was dead, but when he used the past tense, my heart exploded in my chest. With a feral scream, I kicked him squarely in the chest, knocking him onto his back. This time when I flipped him over, no pleading was going to dissuade me.

"One more thing. Does Cookie know that Wren is his half sister?"

McLean looked over his shoulder at me. "If I tell you, will you spare me my life?"

Like hell that was going to happen. I nodded. "Sure."

"Yes. Cookie knew all along that Wren was his sister. He hates her because in his eyes, her mother is the reason that his parents broke up."

I squinted. "So, you're telling me that Cookie, otherwise known as Liam McCrae, took his mother's maiden name? Because it's not Wilson like hers."

"Yes! That's exactly what I'm telling you. He had it legally changed after the divorce was finalized."

"Ha... Good to know," I said, grabbing hold of his collar and pants.

"MacGallan! You said you would spare me my life," he screamed, terror in his eyes.

I lifted a shoulder of indifference. "Yeah. I lied."

This time nothing was stopping me from shoving him face first into the fireplace. As he tries to scramble out, I search his pockets and find a set of keys. Despite him saying that she was dead, I had to see her with my own eyes before I believed him. Placing my foot on his back, it only takes a few minutes for his screams to stop and the flames start to lick along his clothing and then I make my way to the stairs.

Taking three at a time, I stop a moment on the landing and look around. A set of stairs heading to the attic is before me, but doorways stand open down the hallway to my right, and I need to make up my mind quickly as smoke curls up from downstairs. Do I search in each one of them wasting valuable time, or do I go straight for the stairs to the attic? The bastard was gloating, which makes me think he wasn't lying about where Wren is.

I went straight for the stairs, and he was right. The smell of death is heavy. Gagging at the thought of what I might find, I head for the closed door at the top. Fuck! It's locked with a padlock. I call out her name as I try every key on the ring in hopes of some indication that she's still alive. None of the keys work and no sounds come from behind the door. Turning around, I head back down the stairs and enter the room to my left.

It's a bedroom, if you can call it that. A rickety old bed frame sits against one wall, but I walk past it right to the window. The porch roof sits below it, and I waste no time climbing out onto it. Smoke is billowing over the porch roof, and it stings my eyes. But the eastern sky is starting to lighten with the coming dawn, and I'm thankful for it. It reveals a tall pine, uprooted, leaning against the house. The branches sit firmly against the brick, and I discover to my delight, a window. It has to be in the attic. Determined, I start climbing the branches. Paying no heed to the needles piercing my skin, in no time I'm perched outside the window.

It's not big by any means, but big enough for me to get through. I pull the gun from the waist of my jeans and cover my head with my jacket then whack the windowpane with the butt of it. Two hits later, it breaks, and a waft of rotting flesh greets my nostrils. It doesn't stop me. I have to know if she's alive or dead or even if she's here.

Glass digs into my palms as I pull myself over the windowsill and step inside. I don't have time to stand there and pick it out of my skin because the room is filling up with smoke. A door stands closed straight ahead of me and smoke is curling into the attic at the cracks where it meets the frame. The dim light bulb hanging from the ceiling offers little light as I look to my left. There is nothing there but empty boxes and an old steam trunk. I shift my gaze to the right, past the door to the far end of the room, and I end up staring at a dead man chained to a wall. At least I know what the stench is from now, and it's not Wren.

I head back towards the window and place my foot on the sturdiest branch I can find and am following through with my body when I hear coughing coming from inside the room.

I freeze. Dead men don't cough.

I climb back through the window and the smoke

is ten times worse than a few minutes ago. Covering my mouth and nose with my sleeve, I walk over to the man hanging there by his arms. Squatting down in front of him I pull my cell phone out and turn the flashlight on, aiming it at his face. He is definitely gone.

I turn and aim the light around the room and that's when I see her.

Stuffing my phone in my pocket, I rush over to her and cradle her face in my hands. "No, no, no, no! Baby, wake up. Please God, let her wake up."

A crash from downstairs tells me that I don't have time to waste. I look at her wrists, bound by chains and a lock, above her head and my heart sinks because I know that all the keys on the ring in my pocket are too big for the lock.

Just above her hands, I take hold of the chains that are looped through a silver ring. It's attached to a metal plate that is screwed into the wall. Bracing my foot on the floor, I place the other on the wall and pull with every bit of strength I possess. Three screws pop loose, the heads of them flying through the air, but the last one refuses to budge. My arms feel like they are going to be ripped from their sockets, but I don't stop. I can't because I refuse to let the woman I love perish alone in this hell hole.

As the smoke threatens to kill us before the flames, even I must accept defeat. I take a step back, dropping the foot that was braced against the wall. Just when I'm about to join Wren on the floor, so I can hold her as we die together, a set of hands joins mine on the chains. I look over and am relieved that it's Rory standing next to me, his face covered with a bandana.

He yells, "I don't want your job; don't you dare give up."

I nod at him and together we pull. The head of the last screw pops off like it was shot out of a cannon, and I bend to pick up Wren.

Rory shoves me towards the open window. "Get out of here. I'll get her."

Any other time I would have smashed my fist into his mouth. But not this time. My lungs could barely keep up, and I was fading fast. I had to trust him.

I climb out the window and suck in a lungful of breath, and feel heady from the oxygen. Thankfully I recover quickly and go to take Wren from Rory's arms.

"There's a ladder there," he says as he passes her to me.

I shake my head. "That would only work if she were conscious. Get your SUV over here and stand on the roof, I'll hand her down to you."

It felt like an eternity for him to park it as close as he could, but when he did, he wasted no time climbing onto the roof.

Hands outstretched, he grabbed hold of her feet as I dangled her over the edge by her arms. I didn't breathe until she laid safely on top of the roof of his SUV.

Sitting on the edge of the roof of the porch, I turned and placed my hands on the edge and dropped down beside her.

"Come on. Let's get her inside."

Together we got her buckled into the vehicle, and I hurried over to the driver side and got in. I opened the window and closed the door. "Take Jasper back to the estate and see if you can find out where Cookie got off to. By the way, thanks for coming, man. I don't know what I would have done without you."

He grins at me. "Died. You and Wren would have died, Declan."

"No shit." I go to turn the key in the ignition and find it's already forward. "Rory what the fuck is wrong with your car?"

"The alternator is going. Sometimes it works, sometimes it doesn't and when that happens, it doesn't charge the battery."

"For fuck's sake! Get Jasper over here while I get Wren, I'll take her home and have an ambulance meet me there. And call Connor to come give you a boost. And buy yourself a new fucking alternator and a battery while you're at it. God knows I pay you enough."

Chapter 29

Wren

I'm burning up with a fever thanks to the knife wound. McLean should have brought a bigger knife to do the job though because that one hardly made a dent. This was one time I was thankful I had a jelly roll.

I wish I could shift my butt, it's so numb, but I can't. God knows how long I've been chained to this wall. Long enough for my arms to have lost all feeling from sitting on the attic floor in my grandparents' house. Correction was my grandparents' home. They sold it shortly after that Christmas from so long ago. My father or maybe McLean bought it. I don't know, and likely never will, seeing how my father is chained on to the wall opposite me. With his ashen face pointed at the floor and his head lolled to the side, he doesn't look so good. Not good at all. I guess that's what happens when you get shot in the gut and don't get medical attention. You die a slow agonizing death.

If I sound bitter, it's because I am. That man took the one thing from me that I needed most in this life growing up. My mother. Letting me believe that my mother abandoned me. Even now, the tears are slipping down my *cheeks as I remember all the times I'd hated my mother for leaving me. I spit at him and watching it land on his balding head gives me a little shred of satisfaction.*

Instant karma hits me with a flash of pain in my wound, and I giggle for some damn reason. Maybe I'm delirious. I can't have that.

I snap my head up and glance around. An old cardboard box sits a few feet away, and I can see that it is filled with old photographs. Wrapping my hands around the chains, I pull myself up far enough to shimmy my butt back, closer to the wall. Sliding my leg towards the box, it feels like lead when I lift it up and over it then slide the box back towards me.

It's not quite where I want it, right in front of my face would have been nice, but it was close enough that I could peer inside. There had to be at least five hundred photos in the box. A shiver ran up my spine when I focused on the one on top. It was of the house with my grandparent's smiling faces stared back at me from the front porch.

I lift my leg once again, but this time I catch the edge of the box and the photos spill on the floor in front of me. I glance at them, hoping to see my mother. Finally, I see her. Standing in a wedding dress with my father by her side. Both are happy. But there is a looming dark cloud standing right beside my dad, and it's McLean.

How long have they known one another?

A groan from the opposite wall has me looking at my dad. He'd said the debt he'd had with the man had been paid off long before I was born. Debt, not gambling debt like he initially told me.

"Dad!" I yelled.

His head snapped up, and he looked at me. Blood dripped from the corner of his mouth, and I knew from the looks of it, he didn't have much time left.

"Dad! What was the debt you had to pay McLean for?"

His breathing was labored, and I could barely make out his words. "I had to marry your mother," he wheezed. "She was McLean's stepsister and stood to inherit a fortune from her maternal grandmother." He coughed and blood spurted from his lips.

"There's more isn't there?"

He gave a jerky nod. Taking in a shaky breath he continued, "The only way she would receive the money was if she got married. And if she died, McLean got the rest of it. I didn't do it Wren, I wouldn't kill her, I loved your mother."

Confusion spread on my brow. "I know what I heard that night."

"You heard it right. But she wasn't dead, she tripped on her suitcase and hit her head. She didn't want to ruin your Christmas morning, so I called McLean, her brother, to take her to the hospital. He called me later to tell me she died on the way to the hospital." Tears mingled with the blood on his face.

And that's how he died. No goodbye, no I'm sorry, no I love you. He died with a tear-stained face, and I sit here bawling like a baby with so many unanswered questions.

The sound of glass shattering has me flattening myself as best I could against the wall. I duck my head under my arms, trying to see where it's coming from. My vision is blurry, likely from the fever raging through my body, and I blink rapidly, trying desperately to focus them.

I dart my eyes to the door. It's still closed. But a man is standing there, glass at his feet, and it's not registering in my brain that he's standing in front of a window. I watch as he looks around and stops when he sees my dad rotting away. He turns and disappears through the outside wall. It's then that I realize the haze isn't from fever but smoke because I start to choke on it.

I bolt upright and Declan's strong hands come around me. He cradles me to his chest and talks soothingly to me as he trails his hand over my hair and down my arm. "It's okay little goose, you're home. It was just a nightmare. I've got you. Go back to sleep."

My reality has become a recurring nightmare that I keep reliving of my last moments with my dad. His velvety voice soothes me back into a deep sleep, and the next time I awaken is when I feel his head between my legs and his delightful tongue tickles a path over my inner thigh.

This is the first time in 4 weeks that he's touched me so intimately. And I can't wait. It's been a month and a half since I was released from the hospital with strict orders of no 'extracurricular activities. After my knight on horseback, meaning Declan, had raced me back to the estate on Jasper's back, it had done more damage than good and the doctor's feared my knife wound would reopen. Declan took those orders like they were delivered from God himself. No sleeping naked or seeing each other naked. And absolutely no sex.

With bated breath, I wait for him to rip my clothes off and that tongue to swipe across my clit, but it doesn't. Instead, he crawls up my body and lays down beside me. I feel like screaming at him to get down there and do the deed, but a mischievous look in his eye has me stalling.

"What?" I ask when all he does is lay there and stare.

"I handed in my notice yesterday."

I half sit up because he has me thoroughly confused. "Notice of what?"

"Lay back down." He pulls me down to face him, and we lay there looking into each others' eyes. "That I no longer want to be Captain. I'm stepping down. There will need to be another changing of the guard ceremony. But until then, I'll still be in charge."

I laugh. "It's not a job Declan, you can't just quit it."

It's his turn to sit up, and as he does, he tugs the t-shirt that he's wearing over his head. "I'm the Captain. I can and will do whatever I want. And I don't want it, I never did."

Taking his cue, I scurry to a sitting position and strip off my pajama top, tossing it to the floor. "Who will take over? What will you do?"

"Rory. Ideally it would be a blood family member. But seeing how there is only me left in line, he's the only one competent enough to take over." He leaned towards the bedside table and opened the drawer, and took something out, he righted himself and looked at me. "I was thinking of moving to the south of France with my father. There's an old vineyard for sale that I want to try my hand at and a care facility, twenty minutes away that specializes in Alzheimer's and dementia patients that I think would benefit him."

My stomach dropped at his words. He was leaving me.

Chapter 30

Wren

Feeling like a foolish idiot for sitting there with my boobs hanging out while he tells me it's over, I whipped the covers back and swung my legs over the edge of the bed. Tears rolling down my cheeks, I snagged my top from the floor and tried desperately to put it back on.

"What are you doing?" I feel his weight shift on the bed as he hops off. "Little goose! Look at me damnit!"

I stop trying to shove my arm through the sleeve and just sit there with my pajama top covering my face with one arm in, the other at my side. My hand gripping the sheets for dear life while I try to gain some composure that will allow me to walk away from him with my head held high.

But he doesn't allow me that dignity. He pulls the shirt off my head and is standing before me in all his naked glory. With one last look at his magnificent body, my eyes trail over his chiseled chest, down his six-pack stomach to the V of his groin and my eyes narrow.

"When the fuck did you do that?!" Without a thought to the fact that we were over, I raise my hand and trace the raised skin just above his penis that reads *'Property of Little Goose'*.

"When you were taken from me. I went a little off the edge," he stopped for a minute like he was thinking about something, then continued, "Actually, it wasn't a little bit, it was a lot."

I snorted a laugh. "Well, the joke's on you," I nodded my head towards his groin, "That shit's permanent." Not being able to stand another second in this house, I stand up, intent on gathering my belongings.

I sail past him, heading to the bathroom when he says, "As I intended for the woman that I'm asking to marry me."

Spinning around to face him, I look him in the eyes and whisper, "What did you just say?"

I watched with my mouth hanging open because I couldn't believe for a second that this man. This towering naked hunk of a man took to one knee before me and held open up a tiny box between his palms. A pear-shaped diamond winked at me from within the black velvety folds.

Looking at me, like I held his fate in my hands, he said, "Little goose. The woman I love. Put me out of my misery and marry me in the South of France on our vineyard?"

I blubbered out, "Hell yes!"

Leaning my forehead against his, I took his face

between my hands and kissed him. My knight on horseback, my savior.

I hold my hand out for him, and he slips the ring on my finger, and I stare at it as the light catches the fire within.

"It's beautiful Declan," I whisper.

"Not as beautiful as you." He kisses the tip of my nose and smacks my ass. "Get dressed. I have a surprise for you."

I look at him like he's insane. "I thought you wanted to have sex."

He laughed as he walked towards the bathroom. "That can wait. Hurry up and put on some old clothes."

I huffed. "Fine. But it better be good, making me miss out on breakfast sex."

Declan

We enter the sunroom off the kitchen, and I grab a pair of rubber boots off the boot tray. "Put these on."

She gives me the side eye and says, "Why? Are you asking me to clean out the stalls?"

I chuckle. "No. It's muddy out there so you will want to wear them."

As she slips her feet into them, I pull out a blindfold from my back pocket. She looks at it and puts her hand on her hip.

"Declan, what are you doing?"

"Humor me, will you? Turn around."

"Fine." She turns her back to me, and I tie the blindfold around her eyes. Taking her hand in mine, I guided her outside. "Careful of the steps, love."

She giggles as she trips anyway and says, "You have never called me that before. What happened to little goose?"

"Oh, it's still there. You will always be little goose, but you know, sometimes the truth slips out. I do love you."

"Aww. I love you too! You're like the best bad thing that has ever happened to me." She trips going into the barn, but I catch her as she says, "I smell shit. I told you I'm not cleaning stalls."

"Oh, you might after you see your surprise. Take your blindfold off."

She raises her hands and pulls the blindfold down then looks at me. "It's a horse."

I hissed the breath out that I was holding and nodded. "Yeah, she's yours… if you want her." We never did talk about her wanting a horse. Hell, I don't even know if she likes them. But when she jumps on the spot and starts squealing, it's a good guess that she likes her.

"I love her!" She grabs my face in her hands and smacks her lips against mine. "I don't know how to ride though."

I pull her up against me as I dip my hips low and grind them against her as I murmur against her lips, "I'll teach you."

The sound of gravel crunching underfoot tells me that someone is heading towards the barn. "Why don't you introduce yourself to her."

She smiles at me and nods. "Does she have a name?"

"That's for you to decide." I tilt my head towards the horse's rump. "She's already branded."

I watch as she traces her fingertip over the words branded there, just like she did this morning when she saw my identical branding.

"Declan," Rory calls out to me as he approaches the barn. "Got a minute?"

"Give me a minute goose?"

"Sure, take your time," she says. "Abbigail and I are getting acquainted, aren't we girl?"

I step just outside the barn door and look at him. "What's up?"

"We found Cookie."

I rub the stubble on my jaw. "Where is he and what took so fucking long to track him down?"

"Currently he's strapped to a chair in the warehouse downtown." Rory shrugged, "It took time to track him down. He was at his sister's in Dryden Ontario, a fourteen-hour drive from here, in hiding."

I squint at him. "How many siblings does he have?"

"Just this one and Wren."

I shot him a warning look. "Wren doesn't know about him. Is the sister trouble?"

"Sorry." Rory purses his lips then shakes his head. "Nah, she's a librarian or something like that. She's meek, like a mouse."

I take a step back. "Give me an hour."

"Right boss."

Rory walks away, and I head back to Wren in the barn. Realistically, Cookie didn't do a damn thing to Wren other than follow orders. But according to McLean, Cookie hated her. It was time to tell her what was going on.

Wren

This is the first time that Declan and I have had a fight and to say that I won is an understatement. After he informed me of everything that McLean had told him, my first question was, "Why the hell are you just telling me this?!"

His lame excuse was that he was trying to protect me. Yeah right. I threw it in his face that he should have protected me the day I was taken. I immediately felt terrible for saying that and proceeded to tell him what Cookie had done to me. He was livid and pissed that I insisted on going with him to the warehouse.

And that is exactly where we are.

Declan stands to my right and Rory and another

man stand behind on either side of the occupied chair. And I'm standing in front of the man that took great joy backhanding me across my jaw and shoving me to the floor back at my grandparents' house while my hands were tied. My half brother. And I know for a fact the night I escaped the church, if Declan hadn't come along, Cookie would have killed me.

He stares at me and the hatred in his gaze hits me like a brick, and for the life of me, I want to know why.

I walk up to him and yank the duct tape from his mouth.

"You're supposed to be my fucking brother, yet you hate me? Explain yourself," I demand.

"Fuck you." He spits at my feet and Declan takes a step forward, hands clenched into fists at his sides. I throw my arm across his chest. (Some call it the soccer mom save. I call it the granny slap because dear old grannie doesn't know how to put her seatbelt on, and I'm always holding her back from flying through the windshield) then I spit right back into Cookie's face.

"You fucking bitch."

Before I know it, Declan lunges forward and smashes his fist into his mouth. "Apologize to my fiancé."

"Fiancé? Yeah right, Fuck you!"

Declan's fist makes contact again. "I said, apologize."

"Sorry," Cookie mumbles under his breath.

"Remember, I don't leave loose ends." Declan says as

he steps back to stand beside me. "If it were up to me, you would already be dead."

Cookie nods and looks up at me. "What do you want?"

Good question, what do I want?

I took a deep breath. "Why do you hate me?"

"Why do you think? Our father,"— he sneered the word — "wanted nothing to do with us after he met your mother. Do you have any idea what it was like for us? No, you don't. We went from living like kings to trailer park trash. No money for food or clothes, all because of you."

"How is that my fault, that our dad was an asshole? You think living without a father was terrible? Try living without a mother. Do you have any idea what it's like to have to ask a drunk why there is blood coming from your vagina?!"

"Like I care what you had to go through. Declan would have done the world a favor if he'd hit you on the road that night."

I raised my chin. "Well, he didn't, now did he?"

"Give it time." He chuckled. "All you are to him is a piece of ass. He'll drop you once he's bored just like he did with Gretchen."

Despite that sting from his words, I held my hand up and looked at the diamond sparkling on my finger. "Did he give Gretchen a ring? No? I thought not, so shut the hell up about that."

I can feel the tension rising off Declan, he's like a

taut guitar string, ready to snap any second. I glance at him and see a muscle twitching in his jaw from clenching his teeth together. As attractive as that is, I have to wonder if Cookie touched a nerve or if he had given Gretchen a ring.

No. The fucker is trying to drive a wedge between Declan and me, and I won't stand for it.

I look back at my half brother and say, "What's our sister's name?"

"She's not your sister." He glares at me, "Oddly enough, you two are just like one another. Useless, pathetic women. Always has her nose buried in a book and looking to cling to any man that will show her a hint of attention."

"Hmm, perhaps it's because she is trying to escape you." I put my arm around Declan's waist and gave him a squeeze, before sliding my hand back and taking the gun from his waistband. "Maybe I'll help her along."

Raising my arm, I pointed the gun right at him and a blast echoed through the warehouse. With a look of pure shock on his face, he slumped forward, with a bullet between his eyes.

Declan jumped. "Jesus Christ, little goose, you could have given me a warning. I would have done it for you."

"I only meant to scare him!" I dropped the gun like it was a snake and started to shake uncontrollably. "I didn't pull the trigger!"

Declan pulls me into his arms and turns me away from the sight. "Shh, it's okay. Under the right circumstances, everyone is a killer."

I pull back and look him in the eyes. "That may be true but that isn't the case. I'm not a killer, it must have just gone off! I didn't mean to shoot it!"

"You didn't. I did."

Declan and I turn as one and look into the face of my twin. Thinner and a few years older than me but definitely a family resemblance.

"Hello Wren. I'm Mia, your sister."

Declan whips his head to where Rory stands. "Loose ends Rory. What the hell is she doing here?"

The second man that was standing there chuckled and said, "I think Rory and her have a thing for each other."

"Eww," Mia spits out. "No offense Rory!"

Rory's brow creased with a scowl. "Like fuck she does, Senan. She said she wanted to meet Wren. Didn't think any harm in bringing her."

"And what if she was like Cookie and decided to put a bullet in Wren?" Declan dropped his arms from around me and took a step towards Rory.

The second I saw his hand clench into a fist, I grabbed his arm and said, "But she didn't Declan. Let it be."

Epilogue

One month later

"I still don't think Declan trusts me around you," Mia says from behind me as she pins a spray of baby's breath in my hair.

I smooth my hands down the satiny softness of my wedding gown and stare at myself in the mirror. I take a deep breath, hoping to tame the butterflies that are stirring in my stomach. The church is filling up with guests, and in less than an hour, I will be Mrs. Declan Keenan MacGallan. And I cannot wait.

I meet her gaze in the reflection and smile at her. "He's fine. Don't take it personally, he doesn't trust anyone around me."

"Perhaps." She moves back to study her handiwork then says, "I really wish you weren't moving to the South of France, not when we just found each other."

I turn to look at her and take her hands in mine. "I know. I feel the same way. That's why I convinced Declan to go on our honeymoon there first. Just in case we hate it."

She chuckled and pulled me in for a hug. "If I had a chance to move there with a man like Declan, I would jump at it. Please don't stop on my account."

"He is something isn't he?" I smile.

She straightens and looks at me. "He is alright. They are all so damn fine that I would have a hard time picking one. Low key I think Connor is adorable."

I burst out laughing. "Just wait. You're about to be in for a treat!"

"What do you mean?"

An impish grin curves on my lips. "Let's just say, the Irish men have fantastic taste in wedding attire. Just remember when you see him, think of a jaybird."

A knock on the door has us turning to look at it. With a frown on her face, she goes to answer it. "What does that even mean?"

She pulls the door open and there stands Connor in all his Irish finery. "It's time ladies!" He comes into the room, holding his hands out to me, and I take them. "Wren, you look stunning. I'm betting when he sees you, Declan is going to have a hard time hiding his woody."

"Connor!" Mia laughs. "Did you really just say that?"

"I did," he nodded. "It's a bit hard to hide one when wearing a kilt and nothing under it."

A look of horror crosses her face when she looks at me. "Ohmygosh!" she gasps. "That's what you meant by jaybird! Naked as a jaybird, isn't it?!"

I wrinkle my nose and giggle as I loop my arm through hers. "It is. Come on, let's get me married."

Declan

I stand at the altar on my wedding day with my best man beside me, and even though we have been over it a hundred times, I just can't help myself as I watch Wren's sister walk down the aisle carrying flowers with a blush on her face.

I should be elated, which I am. I can't wait for this day to be over. Not that I don't want to marry Wren, far from it. The second I saw her scared on that road, I knew I would protect her for life. But if we had it our way, we would have eloped and be vineyard hopping in the South of France right now. But here we are, at Mia's insistence. Why?

"Rory, did you check to see if Mia has any connections with McLean?" I ask him out of the corner of my mouth as I gaze out over my family sitting in the church pews.

I can feel him rolling his eyes as he sucks in a breath and says, "Yes Declan. I even had my cousin run her through the police wanted list. She's clean. Why do you keep asking?"

"Oh, I don't know. She took care of Cookie without batting an eye,"— I shoot her a tight smile at her as she takes her spot to the right of me— "Wouldn't you say that is questionable?"

He turns and looks me in the eyes and quietly says, "She already told you she's a hunter, and he was a prick to everyone. She did us a favor."— he stepped back in line beside me— "Don't worry Declan, after the changing of the guard ceremony I'll make sure to keep her close."

The wedding march started playing, and I gave him a curt nod. "Be sure she doesn't leave." And then the air in my lungs lodged itself in my throat as Wren came into view. My father on one side of her and Connor on the other. She insisted that they both give her away.

Tears sting my eyes as her gaze seeks me out, and I can finally breathe again when she smiles at me. I watch, my eyes only for her, and I am mesmerized with every step she takes.

I guess Mia was right about one thing. If we had eloped, we would have robbed ourselves of this moment.

She stops beside me, and I offer her my arm and together we turn to look at the clergyman.

"Who gives this woman away?"

"We do," my dad and Connor say at the same time.

The clergyman nods and begins the ceremony.

As Wren says her vows, and slips my wedding ring on my finger, everything seems to pass in a daze until Rory is shoving her wedding band into my hand and the Clergyman is saying my name.

"Declan wishes to say something."

Wren looks at me with a look of pure anxiety and confusion because we had decided that we would just use the traditional vows. But I had other plans.

I lean towards her and brush my lips against her temple, "It's okay, bare with me."

Standing straight, I take her hand in mine and clear my throat, and as I slip the ring on her finger I say,

"Little Goose. From the moment you flew out of the trees and landed in front of my car, you've tormented me. Healed me. Amazed me. Mesmerized me. Captivated me. And crossed me in ways that no other human dares to. I fall in love with you more every morning and every night. You are the air to my lungs, and I will protect you until my dying breath. I take you, Wren Christina Wilson, as my wife."

Tears slip down her cheeks, and I wipe them away as the clergyman says, "As you stand before us and God, you have kissed many times. Perhaps a thousand, but today, you get to kiss as husband and wife. Please kiss your bride."

He didn't have to tell me twice.

the end

Keep reading for a look into Salvation Rory and Kat's story.

SAVIOR

Chapter 1

Rory Hennessey

My balls are freezing. Standing around in a kilt is not my idea of a good time.

Not when there is a cool wind whipping around and at any given moment the ladies across from me will get an eyeful. It's bad enough that they are sitting there in chairs across the dance floor, eye fucking me as I lean against a tent pole, holding my damn skirt down.

Ignoring them, I scowl at the people dancing around at my best friend's wedding reception and can't help but wonder why the hell I'm still here. Sure, I was the best man, but that duty was done hours ago.

I'm happy for the couple though. Declan, marrying Wren, a woman he found in the middle of a road after she ran off from her arranged marriage, is definitely his match. But for some strange reason, part of me is not happy. I think it's because Declan announced he was stepping back as Captain of the clan. As Clan Chief, the second in command, I'm to take his place. Something I don't want.

"Care to dance?"

I turn to see one of the women, a blonde with fake tits, from across the way, standing to my right. She's a brave one.

I shake my head. "I'm good."

Her face falls, and I feel like an ass for being such a jerk. "Fine!"

I take hold of her hand and drag her on to the dance floor. Pulling her into my arms, she bumps her forehead against my chin, and my head whips back. Fuck, I grit my teeth and smile at her. I shouldn't have done that because now she wants to talk.

"What's your name?" she asks.

I look down at her. I must have a scowl on my face because she says, "Never mind."

Which is fine by me. We dance in silence, and the song is coming to an end when I feel a tap on my shoulder. I turn to see Ian, the stable hand standing there white as a ghost. I drop my arms from around the blonde and turn my full attention to the kid.

"What is it?"

"Tomas, he was out at the barn, and before I knew it, got into the pasture and climbed onto a cow's back."

"I thought you were taking him to the house. How the hell did he get out to the barn?"

"I did. But after he changed into his robe, he insisted on going out to the barn. For an old man, he's damn quick. Anyway, the cow took off and he fell, hit his head, blood was everywhere, and for a minute, I thought he was dead."

"Jesus Christ. Call an ambulance." My eyes search out Declan. He is dancing with Wren, as if there isn't another soul in the room, and I make my way over to them as Ian trails behind.

"I already did, they are on their way. I covered him with a blanket, and Charlie is with him right now," he said.

"Good."

I tap Declan on the shoulder, and he mutters, "Not now."

I lean close and say, "Your dad is laying in the pasture, he fell off a cow."

Declan lifted his head and looked at me.

"What the fuck did you just say?"

"The ambulance is on its way."

The next day, we are standing in the office looking at the security camera footage of Tomas sneaking out into the pasture in his bathrobe. The doctors are claiming that the farm is not a suitable home for Tomas and want to put him into a nursing home.

"You know, this is only going to prove that Tomas was unsupervised," I say, squinting at the screen.

"Maybe. Just watch. See if either of you can find

Ian just out of frame," Declan murmurs, eyes on the screen.

He stands on a watering trough, looks around and when he sees that the coast is clear, he grabs onto the heifers' ears and pulls himself onto her back.

"What a sneaky little bugger," Wren mumbles.

For a full ten seconds, Tomas can be seen kicking his heels into her sides, she takes a few steps but then bolts and Tomas bounces then flips over her butt, his ass crack and family jewels, captured in the still frame as Declan hits the keyboard and turns around to look at us.

I hit the enter key and rewind it, letting it play and burst out laughing. "He got some pretty good air there."

I clamp my mouth shut when Declan gives me a murderous look. "Yeah, and no Ian. We need to find those papers."

"I don't understand why you need to prove that you are power of attorney Declan," Wren said as she shuffled through a stack of papers on the desk. "He's your dad."

I head over to the chair I had vacated and sit down, looking through the box I'd left there while Declan sits behind the desk rubbing his forehead. We've been at it for hours until we watched the footage, searching in every box and filing cabinet for the proof that he is power of attorney but it's like looking for a needle in a haystack.

"Doesn't matter if I'm his son when it comes to the Doctors, I have no say. He could be placed anywhere in Ontario that has the first bed available. With that paper it proves I legally have the say and can bring him home and hire a nurse to care for him."

Done with the box, I set it down on the floor beside me and stood, "What about calling the lawyer, wouldn't he have a copy?"

Declan pushes his chair back and disappears under the desk. "Thought of that. But he's long dead."

"What are you doing down there?" Wren asks, as she stacks the papers into a neat pile.

I move around the desk, thinking my friend has finally lost it to see him looking at the underside of the desk. Wren joins me and together we watch.

"When I was a kid, I would always hide under here. My dad would yell at me and tell me to get the fuck out"— he runs his fingers along the corners, feeling for something— "I never knew why until one day, I was hiding behind the curtains when he came in. There you are, you little bastard."

We watch as he presses his finger into the wood as if it were melted butter and a tiny drawer pops out. He pulls a key from within, and we move back as he crawls out.

"What is that for?" Wren asks, as she looks at the key in the palm of his hand.

"A safe," he said, looking around the room. "I just don't know where it is. Start searching behind everything."

"If you saw that he had the key, wouldn't you have seen where the safe was?" I ask as we spread out, each heading to a picture on the wall.

He shakes his head as he looks behind a painting of his dad. "No. He saw the curtains move and kicked me out of the room."

"Then what makes you think it's for a safe?" Wren asked as she lifted a mirror off the wall.

Declan shrugged. "I don't, but what else could it be for?"

With that thought we checked behind every obvious place. After a few minutes, I stand there with my hands on my hips eyeing the room as Wren and Declan roll up a Persian rug.

I turn and look at him. "Declan, what has been in this room since you were a kid?"

He stands up and glances around. "That gold horse and that plant," he points at each of them.

Wren takes the plant, and Declan and I go over to the horse, the size of a Shetland pony and knock on it. "This thing is solid! Is it real gold?"

"I don't know," Declan shrugged. "The story I was told growing up was that it was from some heist in England back in the 80's. The bars were melted down and poured into casts shaped like animals. My dad was a liar too, so it's hard to tell really."

I take the head of the horse and lift it. It barely comes off the floor. "Fuck me, it has to weigh close to four hundred pounds. If it is real this would be worth —"

"In the billions," Delcan nods. "And that's why it's still here." He grabs the ass end and looks at me. "Ready?"

I take hold of the head and nod.

"How the hell did Tomas get this here?" I say through gritted teeth as we lift it.

Declan grunts. "Knowing him, he built the damn house around it."

Winded, we set it aside. And right there under the damn golden horse is the door to an old safe.

Squatting, Declan pulls the key out of the pocket of his jeans and fits it into the keyhole. He turns it and pulls on the handle and the door swings open.

He pulls out a bag of diamonds and they twinkle in the day light as he sets them on the floor, and I have to wonder how many years it's been since sunshine played along their surface. Next, he pulls out a manilla envelope and Wren takes that from him. She sits on the floor and starts going through each paper. "Aha! Here it is," she grins as she hands it to Declan.

"Thank you!" he says, as he grabs her and pulls her into his arms.

While they get down and dirty, I clear my throat because clearly, they forgot that I am in the room, and they pull apart looking guiltily at me.

Wren giggles. "Sorry," she says, smoothing her hair in place. "What about the rest of the stuff in the safe?"

"Might as well go through it," Declan says, handing me a box with flowers on it. "See what's in that, while I count how many stacks of cash the old man had hidden in here."

I lift the lid of the box to find a stack of photos of a young woman staring up at me. Pulling them out, I'm halfway through looking at them when I realized they are of the same girl. I hold out the latest photo to Declan and say, "Who is this?"

He takes it from me and studies it. "Hell, if I know. Is that all that's in the box, pictures of this girl?"

I shake my head as I look at a stack of letters. Looks to be love letters if the flowery scent is any indication. "These." I hold them up.

Wren wrinkles her nose. "What's that smell? It smells like Chantilly Lace." She takes the letters from me and starts sniffing them. "Oh my god it is! My mother used to wear this perfume. What else is in there?"

I shuffle through the box and start calling out everything I see. "A receipt from Sears, a copy of someone's birth certificate, a paternity test—"

"A what?!" Declan and Wren say at the same time.

I start to repeat myself when Declan says, "We heard you the first time. Let me see that."

He takes the box from me and starts going through it. I watch as he takes the paternity test and starts to read it. He looks right at me. "Son of a bitch. You know what this means don't you?"

Wren shakes her head as I say, "No?"

He looks stunned. "It means that this girl, woman, whatever, Katrina George is my half sister. My dad is her dad."

"That's awesome!" Wren claps her hands. "Now I have a sister-in-law."

Declan shakes his head. "No, it's not Wren. It's not awesome. It means that she's blood, and she can take over the spot as Captain."

"How? She knows nothing about the family," I say in disbelief.

"She's blood Rory," he says. "It always passes to blood if they want it. None of my cousins did, I don't blame them, they all have successful careers, no one wanted it. That's why it will pass to you or would if she doesn't want it."

Wren takes a paper from the box and holds it up. "Her mother's name is Dahlia and here's her phone number."

I snatched it from her and pulled out my phone from my back pocket. I didn't want the position of Captain, but sure as shit, I wasn't allowing an outsider to take over, especially a woman.

I punched the number into my phone and waited, hand on my hip for her to answer. She picked up the fifth ring.

A soft, "Hello?" sounded in my ear.

"Who the fuck is this?"

"Excuse me? Who the fuck is this? You are the one who called me!"

"That's beside the point. Now tell me who you are."

"Go fuck yourself."

The phone made a noise, and I looked at it, scowling. "She hung up on me!"

"Give me that!" Wren stood up and snatched the phone out of my hands. "Do you blame her?"

You can get your copy of Rory's story, Salvation right here

Other books by Aquila Thorne

CHANGING OF THE GUARDS
SAVIOR

SALVATION

SANCTUARY

BLINDSIDED

Related to the Changing of the Guards

LILY AND HER MERCENARY

EDEN AND HER MERCENARY

PEARL LAKE SERIES

MOONLIT NIGHT AND MOONLIT STALKER

MOONLIT ROAD

HEAVEN IN THE MOONLIGHT

THE INN AT PEARL LAKE

LANE'S DESTINY

TIM' BAR

HER CHRISTMAS WISH

THE BLOOD MOON SERIES

THE SUMMONS

HEAVEN AND HELL

HUNTING THE OMEGA

Printed in Dunstable, United Kingdom